FLYING
in love

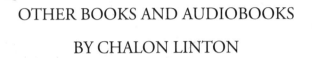

OTHER BOOKS AND AUDIOBOOKS

BY CHALON LINTON

FLYING *in love*

an air force romance

CHALON LINTON

Covenant Communications, Inc.

Cover images: *Pure Magic* © SrdjanPav / istockphoto.com. *U.S. Air Force Cargo Airplane above the Clouds* © Ivan Cholakov / shutterstock.com.

Cover design by Aleesa Parsons © 2020 by Covenant Communications, Inc.

Published by Covenant Communications, Inc.
American Fork, Utah

Printed in the United States of America
First Printing: June 2020

26 25 24 23 22 21 20   10 9 8 7 6 5 4 3 2 1

ISBN 978-1-52441-305-7

To the spouses who support their military members
through peacetime and war

PRAISE FOR
Chalon Linton

FLYING IN LOVE

"Linton (*Adoring Abigail*) brings a chaste Regency sensibility to this tender contemporary military romance . . . Paige's crisp narrative voice and the charming chapter titles . . . create the effect of reading through a good friend's blog. Sweet without being cloying, this is sure to appeal to fans of *G*-rated romance."

—*Publishers Weekly*

"*Flying In Love* is one of the sweetest, most sincere, most tender romances I've read in a long time. Skillfully penned, the layered characters take up residence firmly in your heart, and watching these two broken-but-delightful people fall in love will leave that same heart sighing happily. I alternated between grinning and brushing away a few tears . . . but mostly grinning. Highly recommended!"

—Carrie Schmidt, ReadingIsMySuperPower.org

"*Flying in Love* is a sweet romance about faith, trust, and finding that special someone who creates balance in your life. This is a perfect read for the beach or a lazy weekend."

—Sarah Alva, author of *The Doctor and the Midwife* (coming September 2020)

"A book rarely keeps me up all night, but this one did. Ms. Linton's well-developed character arcs and realistic portrayal of military life came together seamlessly in this Christian contemporary romance. A definite must-read! Bravo."

—Paige Edwards, author of *Catherine's Intrigue* & *Deadly by Design*

"In *Flying in Love*, author Chalon Linton captivates readers with a heartwarming contemporary romance filled with heartbreak, loss, and discovering true love . . . The author's own background of being a military spouse adds authenticity to the story. The author shares the message of God's love and faithfulness and the power of prayer for comfort and peace. *Flying in Love* is recommended for readers of contemporary romance."

—Nicole, InkwellInspirations.com

ADORING ABIGAIL

"Linton (*Escape to Everly Manor*) elevates this straightforward Regency romance with self-actualized protagonists and a fine eye for historic detail. Robert's acceptance of Abigail's difference is instant and heartwarming, but Linton wisely avoids 'cured by love' clichés, instead painting a sensitive portrait of Abigail's growing belief in herself. This uplifting story is sure to gratify readers of chaste romance."

—*Publishers Weekly*

"Highly recommend!"

—Midwest Book Review

"I found their relationship and struggles fresh, and I couldn't help but cheer for them. I ended up really enjoying the book. Worth reading!"

—Carolyn Twede Frank, author *Under the Stars*

"5 stars hands down! I've read this author before, and I liked her style of writing even then. [Linton] manages to pull you into the book from the beginning until the end."

—Redheadedbooklady

"A sweet romance that will make your heart happy."
—Julie Coulter Bellon, author (*The Marquess Meets His Match*)

ACKNOWLEDGMENTS

FLYING IN LOVE HAS BEEN waiting a very long time to land in the hands of readers. So many facets came together to bring this story to press. First and foremost, to my fellow military spouses, you are strong and amazing, and I pray you can see the humor, reality, and hope in this story. While our spouses may be the ones reporting for duty, we are a military family and ride this road together. We have met such wonderful people in every part of our military journey, and I thank you for the shared hugs, tears, and laughter.

Thank you to the team at Covenant Communications: Kami Hancock, Amy Parker, and Aleesa Parsons, plus the many other dedicated employees who work behind the scenes to create the finished book and audiobook. The Covenant team champions my book from the moment of submission through the design, marketing, and promotion and gives more than I could ask for.

When my husband was sworn in all those years ago, we could not have imagined the path our lives would take. We have been blessed in our safety, our assignments, and our friendships. As a little girl, I never considered I would be a military spouse. There have been rough times and great adventures, and I would not change a thing.

Flying in Love is a fictional romance written with the input of military members and their spouses. Please forgive any inaccurate representation or information. And no matter your political affiliation, please support the men and women in uniform and their families as they dedicate themselves to defend freedom. May God bless America.

CHAPTER 1
I Ran

THE THUDDING IN MY FEET matched the drumming in my head. I swiped the tears from my eyes and noticed a flickering gas station sign. The vice on my lungs tightened. The pain screamed for me to stop, but I couldn't. If I stopped, I had to think, had to remember, and the last thing I wanted to do was remember.

For ten months Gavin and I had dated. For ten months I had devoted everything to him. My time. My attention. My heart. Things had progressed well, or so I had thought.

Today, after a long day at work, I headed straight for the gym. After my workout, I thought it would be fun to grab takeout and surprise Gavin. He'd texted earlier telling me he landed the huge account he'd been vying for. I texted back that we should celebrate. I knew he didn't like surprises, but I felt justified. Besides, it wasn't a secret birthday party or a surprise date; it was only dinner. I assumed my thoughtful gesture would make him happy.

Gavin didn't answer my knock, but I heard music playing out back. He often lifted free weights in his backyard while blaring whichever crazy punk band he was currently fixated on. I left the box of food at the front door, shoved my keys and phone into the pocket of my hoodie, and went to find him. Perhaps I should have realized this music was different. Perhaps I should have noticed the unfamiliar car parked on the street. Perhaps, when the door remained closed, I should have walked away, but I didn't. Instead I walked around the side yard of the house, intending to enter through Gavin's back gate. Stupidly, I set myself up.

The six-foot privacy fence concealed my presence. I smiled and pictured Gavin's reaction when I popped my head over the fence. He would be glad to see me, grateful for a break in his workout. He would unlock the gate and scoop me into a sweaty hug. I couldn't wait.

But I should have.

The song drifted to an end, and in the beat before the next one started, I heard an unfamiliar sultry laugh, followed by Gavin's deep voice. I didn't hear what was said, but I halted near the back corner of the property.

The implications eluded me. My mind functioned with the glass-is-half-full mentality. Hearing a woman's voice didn't mean anything, but now I was curious. I pushed up onto my tippy-toes, to no avail. My work heels might have given me the leverage I needed, but my workout shoes offered only another half inch at most to my five-seven frame. Surveying the options, I decided the boulder lining the running trail would be ideal. I easily stepped on top and looked into Gavin's yard.

I noticed three things. First, Gavin was not working out. Second, he sat decidedly close to a petite brunette and smiled at something she said. Third, used dishes and utensils were scattered on the patio table, along with two lit candles.

While I consider myself an intelligent individual, the optic nerves in my head must have been misfiring, because I still didn't doubt Gavin, nor my relationship with him. I decided he was celebrating with a coworker or welcoming a cousin to town or . . . I didn't know what. But I was ready to find out. I glanced at the ground to determine where to jump, and when I looked back up, the movement of Gavin and the brunette coming together pulled my eyes back to the yard, where I had a front-row seat to their very passionate, very long, and very indulgent kiss.

The moment collided in my brain like a super zoom on a high-tech camera, and I realized, standing on the boulder with tears in my eyes, that I was part of the scene—a scene I wanted nothing to do with—so I ran.

I passed the gas station and punched the button on the crosswalk over and over and over until the beeping began with the change of the signal. I couldn't feel my heartbreak, because I chose to torture my lungs instead. While my body screamed out in pain, my brain kicked into full operation. I replayed the scene in my mind, only this time I high-jumped over the fence and knocked their heads together, laughing the entire time. My lips curved up as I considered smearing the burritos I had brought for dinner all over Gavin's front door. I remembered the unfamiliar car and considered letting the air out of the woman's tires. But darn the kind, responsible, considerate side of me—what if it wasn't her car and I released my fury on some poor old man? But I did know Gavin's car, and I could wreak havoc on his precious BMW.

I turned off the main road and wound into suburban paradise. Everything was too perfect: the lawns, the houses, and the stupid fall wreaths hanging on the doors. I stopped abruptly and screamed, then sobbed with my head in my hands. Surely someone would call the police. I could blame my first run-in with the law on my cheating boyfriend.

When they arrived, I would explain why it hurt so bad. I would tell them how Gavin and I met at Millie's Café. I was a regular there, and one day I'd sat clicking away on my laptop but had taken a moment to enjoy a sip of my specially made caramel cinnamon hot chocolate. I had savored every swallow, and Gavin had watched the corners of my mouth turn up at the delicious caramel bliss as I cradled the pale-blue mug in my hands. He'd wondered what drink could inspire such ecstasy, so he walked over and asked. We hit it off, talking for almost two hours, and left with each other's phone number.

He had called the next day and asked me to dinner. We'd been dating exclusively since then. At least, I had been exclusive.

Ten entire months. We'd been casual, taken things slowly. His kisses were intoxicating but also precious.

The moment I'd turned thirteen, Mom had hounded me with talks about promiscuity and saving myself for marriage. "We Christians have to set an example," she'd said. I'd sat beside Mom on our family pew for as long as I can remember. Every time I dated someone new, she'd repeated the doctrine. I knew she was right. I believed in the sanctity of marriage. I just wished she could give me a little credit. I was twenty-five years old, after all. I'd set boundaries with Gavin, and kissing served as the outer limit. We'd saved our kisses for the opportune times so things would never push too far. With these limits, Gavin had expressed himself in other ways, and my insides tingled from the simple things: his name lighting up my phone, a text to tell me he was thinking about me, a wink—Gavin winked at me a lot, and his lips would turn up in the most adorable, teasing grin.

I knew how I felt about him. I'd known since the first month. I liked him. A lot. I could see a future together. A forever kind of future with a house, kids, and a happily ever after. We'd never talked about the forever part, but we did talk about next month and even next year.

Gavin hadn't wasted an opportunity to tell me how great I was or how he appreciated me, and he'd often called me gorgeous. Then, *yesterday*, Gavin did it. He'd taken things further. Standing on my front porch, he'd held me in one of the great hugs only Gavin could give. He'd inhaled my mango shampoo and sighed. Then he'd said, "I love you, Paige Hall."

I'd melted in his arms.

Only twenty-four hours ago he'd said the words I'd waited ten months to hear. Words that now felt hollow and broken, empty and fabricated. Words I never wanted to hear from him again.

CHAPTER 2
I Wept

THANKFULLY, THE POLICE WERE NOT called. The sun set, and I found a small park tucked in among the houses. It was empty, so I claimed it as my own and wept.

After a long while, my tears dried. I considered what I felt and attributed my discomfort to my broken heart. My chest squeezed tight. I supposed it could be pain from my heart, yet I had also pounded out at least seven grueling miles. Maybe my lungs were protesting the effort I'd extracted from them.

I tasted the salt tears on my lips, and the bitter taste unleashed a new emotion—anger. Gavin didn't deserve to be cried over. He didn't deserve my tears. My body should not ache due to anything in relation to him. I gave a definitive nod and decided then and there that the cheater he'd turned out to be would not affect me again.

When I stood, my legs cramped, and I groaned as I looked at the sky and remembered that my car was parked at Gavin's house. I pulled out my phone, both cautious and curious as to what messages I might find. Nothing. Figured.

I called Mandy. After Gavin's confession of his feelings the night before, Mandy had listened to me recount the hug and accompanying declaration a handful of times. I'd dissected each point of contact, each breath, and she'd patiently indulged me until she could no longer muffle her yawn.

Calling her now and confessing the polar opposite was humiliating. But if anyone could understand, it would be her.

"Hey, Paige," she answered cheerfully.

I remained silent for a moment, tears burning again in my eyes. "Hi," I finally said.

She knew me too well. "What's wrong?"

I blinked, and the tears fell. I hit my fist into my thigh and growled at the fact that I could not steady my voice. "Can you come pick me up?"

I heard movement on Mandy's end. "Of course, but you're scaring me. What happened? Where are you?"

"I don't even know," I answered and walked toward the sidewalk, hoping to find a street sign.

"Don't know where you are? Or don't know what happened?"

"Either."

"Paige? What's going on?"

"Gavin . . ."

"Oh no! Is he hurt?"

I actually laughed. "He's fine. Great. Dandy!" I pulled my hair tie out and let my long dark-brown hair fall around my shoulders.

"Paige?"

"He's so dandy that when I stopped by to bring him dinner tonight, he had already eaten. At his house. With another woman. And followed up with *dessert*," I said, sensually sounding out the last word.

"As in . . ."

"Yes, face-smacking with said woman." My chest hurt again, and emotions constricted my throat, forcing quick breaths.

"Ah man, Paige." Mandy sighed. "I don't know what to say."

I took a shaky breath. "Can you come?" I asked.

I gave her the names of the cross streets, and she pulled up twenty minutes later. She leaned across the passenger seat and pushed the door open for me.

"I stopped by Jason's on the way over and gave him your extra set of keys. He's going with his roommate to pick up your car," she said.

"Thanks." I leaned my head back on the headrest and pressed my fingertips against my eyelids. "I really didn't want to have to go get it."

"I figured. I also figured I didn't need to ask what flavor custard you wanted at Millie's, so I called in our order." Mandy leaned over the console and wrapped me in an awkward hug. "Come here."

I controlled my sniffles, but the faucet of tears opened again. I sighed and wiped the moisture from my face. "Can we go already?" I asked.

"Sure thing." Mandy drove to Millie's and left me and my puffy eyes in the car while she paid for the custard. Then she drove to the rental house we shared.

I plopped down on the couch, and she let me eat silently until her brother returned and dropped off my car keys. When Jason left, I gave Mandy the play-by-play, and she gasped and aahed and offered to go slit Gavin's tires at all the correct times.

The flood of tears tempered and released on a crazy-precise fifteen-minute cycle until I had a throbbing headache that even chocolate custard with pecans and caramel could not cure. Mandy gave me a hug again, filled with enough pity and Gavin-is-a-jerk emotion to get me through the night. I shuffled my sore legs to bed, closed my swollen eyes, and fell directly to sleep.

People live in California for the temperate climate, but fall mornings should not be filled with bright sunshine-lit skies. Even in California, fall skies should be gray and dull and mopey. I managed work the next day by staying in my classroom and avoiding any stops in the front office. Weekends were always a boon, but this one was even more so. In my morning prayer, I expressly thanked God that it was a Friday. I planned to hunker down in my room, burn anything Gavin related, and binge watch the Colin Firth version of *Pride and Prejudice*. Mr. Darcy would never listen to a punk band.

Gavin had to know he'd been busted. He never outright admitted it, but late last night he did text and ask if I'd brought food by. When I didn't respond, he'd texted again, asking if I was okay. Today he had tried to call or text about once an hour until I responded with a text, asking him not to call me ever again. I hesitated for only a minute, wondering if I was acting too extremely, but I knew I wasn't. He'd cheated. He'd lied. Plain and simple. I refused to let him back in.

But pushing him out left a gaping hole inside of me. Not only did I feel empty but I also sensed this giant vortex sucking everything good away from me. On the drive to work, I'd passed various businesses or streets I associated with a memory of Gavin. A song on the radio, the smell of a coworker's cologne, a particular food or phrase, even the plate in my cupboard that was chipped because Gavin had decided to demonstrate his musical skills and realized too late that a plate and a cast-iron lid weren't a good combination for cymbals—all things led back to Gavin.

Gavin stopped by my house on Saturday and asked to talk to me. Mandy made me proud. I listened in my room while she gnawed him up and down and told him to leave me alone.

"I made a stupid mistake." Gavin pleaded, "Please, Mandy, let me talk to her."

The chisel drove further into the crack in my heart, and I wanted the pain to stop. I considered facing him. For a moment I wondered if it was true. Was he sorry? Did he want me back? Could I go back?

Thankfully, Mandy ended my doubt when she said, "Gavin, she's too good for you. She's always been too good for you."

It was quiet for a moment.

"I know," he said.

And then he left.

Mandy saved me from myself, and I was grateful I had stayed in my room.

By Sunday Gavin stopped texting and calling. On Monday a dozen red roses were delivered to my school. The secretary thought they were so beautiful that she brought them straight to my room. The card simply said, *I'm sorry. Gavin.* I tossed the card into the trash can. I was sorry too. It was over.

CHAPTER 3
I paused

THE WEEK PASSED SLOWLY, AND every day I considered throwing the roses away. The bouquet bloomed in perfection, and the fragrant scent lent a melodramatic flair to my moping. By the time Friday rolled back around, I knew I needed a few days filled with distractions only my niece and nephews could provide. My only sister, Heather, lived an hour away, so I headed to her house after school. I needed to hit the pause button on my life and consider what God had in store for me. Goodness surrounded me, though when the heartbreak hit too hard, it was difficult to remember that.

Heather was welcoming, sympathetic, and accommodating. After my initial telling of events (which somehow seemed less dramatic because I didn't tell her about Gavin's confession of love), I asked Heather not to mention his name or his smile or his amazing chocolate eyes. She and her husband, Greg, obliged me one hundred percent. Two-year-old Max and five-month-old Nathaniel were too young to connect Gavin to my mopey mood. But my four-year-old niece, Amelia . . . not so much. And I couldn't blame her for wanting to see Mr. Gavin so he could give her another roller-coaster ride. Her favorite game had been to sit on Gavin's knees and hold his hands while he moved his legs from side to side, pretending like he would shake her off. The mechanical clicks and sounds he made with his mouth, trying to simulate a creaky old ride, were pretty entertaining. I think Amelia knew the experience of holding Gavin's hand was pretty awesome. She asked me to take his place in their make-believe roller-coaster game, but I couldn't go there. Not even for Amelia. So instead I employed her in a new game: a very dramatic rendition of ring-around-the-rosy.

I also convinced Heather to back me up while I called my mother, so she made me a cup of cocoa and sat with me on the back porch while Greg put the kids to bed. Mom loved Gavin almost as much as I did, but our feelings no longer mattered.

"Get it over with," Heather said and reached her hand out for my phone. I complied, and before I could delay further, she dialed Mom's number and handed my phone back.

By the third ring, I hoped Mom wouldn't answer, and I noticed Heather had pulled out her tablet. I whimpered and asked Heather if she wanted to trade places, but before she could respond, Mom picked up.

"You're alive! When none of my messages were returned, I thought I'd lost my second child," Mom said. Her snarky comment was not a point in my favor.

Heather, my younger brother, Matt, and I had dissected Mom's attempted humor. When my mom relaxed, she could get all of us laughing to the point of tears. When she wanted, her talent was honed and mastered. Unfortunately, when she was hurt or frustrated, she tried to apply biting sarcasm, and those quips never went over quite right.

I knew if I didn't play along, Mom would get defensive. Things would only be worse once I explained why I had avoided talking with her for the last week. She was confident in so many things, but she kept her emotions hidden away, supplementing jokes for any real feeling while thriving on knowing my every sentiment. My emotions resembled more of a billboard. I liked displaying my true self. Riddles had never been my forte.

The Band-Aid had to come off. I took a deep breath and apologized to Mom for not getting back with her. Then I rambled through the reason behind my terrible week.

"You broke up with Gavin?" Mom asked.

I held the phone away from my ear and rolled my eyes at Heather. She gave me two thumbs up, which may have worked to encourage Amelia to clean her room but did nothing to boost my confidence.

Moving the phone back into place, I said, "I saw him kissing someone else. Of course I broke up with him."

"Maybe there's a good explanation. Are you sure it wasn't his sister?"

"Really, Mom? I've met his sister, and—it wasn't a sisterly sort of kiss."

"Then, who was it?" she pressed.

I sighed. "I don't know, and to be honest, I don't care. It wasn't me, which is all that matters."

"Oh, honey, I'm sorry," Mom said. She paused, and I braced for the deluge. The flood of comments did not disappoint. "What did Gavin have to say for himself? Do I need to talk to that young man? How dare he disrespect my daughter in such a way! How did you catch this man-stealer kissing him? Have you considered counseling? Are you sure you want to break up? What have you done since you found out? Does his mother know what kind of son she raised?"

I waited until the floodwaters dissipated, and then I said, "Mom, Gavin hurt me. It's been a hard week, and I don't want to relive it over and ov—"

"I'm not asking you to relive it," she cut in. "I just wanted to know if he's sorry. I mean, could you trust him not to do it again, or—?"

"Mom," I snapped. "I don't want to talk about it anymore. This is exactly why I didn't call." The silence on the other end effectively ignited my guilt. Heather set her tablet aside and put her hand on my arm. Tears sprang to my eyes. "Mom," I said. "I'm sorry. It's just that he really hurt me, and I'm ready to move on."

"I'm only trying to help," Mom mumbled into the phone. Then she laughed and said, "Heather and I will hold his arms, and you can throw sand in his eyes." She laughed again. "Then he'll know how badly he hurt you."

I'd take sand in my eyes any day—sand washes out. I didn't know when I'd be able to cleanse myself from the ache that had taken up residence in my heart.

"Mom, I don't want to hurt him. I just don't want to see him again."

"Well," Mom said, "you know the saying 'When something seems too good to be true, it probably is.'"

"You make it sound as if Gavin's perfect, and if there's one thing I've realized since last Thursday, it's that Gavin is definitely not perfect."

"Well, maybe this is God's way of telling you He has another plan in store," Mom said.

"Maybe," I said. I only wished God would have let me know about this alternate plan ten months ago.

I hung up with Mom, and without a word, Heather leaned over and gave me a hug. "Let's go get a refill on our cocoa and watch a movie," she said.

After a tight squeeze, I released my hold on her. "As long as it's a cartoon or a flick with a crazy psychopath killer. No romance!"

"Ah, come on, sis. 'What are men compared to rocks and mountains?'" Heather said, dramatically quoting one of my favorite Jane Austen lines. "Couldn't you use a little Mr. Darcy?" Heather asked as I followed her back to the kitchen.

"I could use a lot of Mr. Darcy," I mused.

I'd gifted Heather the Matthew Macfadyen version of *Pride and Prejudice* a few years back. I figured, with three kids, stealing two hours away to get an Austen fix would be easier than the six hours required for my preferred BBC version of the movie. Mr. Darcy, no matter the actor, is always an ideal distraction. But what was Jane Austen thinking? She'd ruined the entire male species when she created that man. Fitzwilliam Darcy is truly perfection personified.

I spent the rest of the weekend entertaining Max, who liked to climb everything, and snuggling Nathaniel. Throw in my sister's homemade melt-in-the-mouth chocolate-chip butterscotch cookies, and I considered the weekend to be a relative success.

Monday morning arrived, and I actually boasted a sincere smile as I walked into work. After chatting with the office staff, I moved to my room down the hall. There were about thirty-five students who qualified for speech therapy, and I didn't need an entire classroom. Instead I'd been given a large workroom with enough space for two circular desks to serve as workstations, a small table for a listening center, and my small teacher's desk, which sat cozily in the corner. On my desk I discovered the card Gavin had sent with the flowers.

Miranda, the attendance clerk, walked by and waved. She must have noticed my strained expression, because she stopped midstep and put her hand on the doorframe. "Hey, I fished that out of the trash for you. I figured it was important."

My heart clenched, and it took a lot of restraint not to yell. I faked a smile along with a word of gratitude, and Miranda left. I should have known my healing wasn't complete. One weekend could not undo ten months of Gavin.

After work I needed groceries. Gavin and I had made a habit of shopping together, and I knew he often stocked up on Mondays after work. I could not run into him. I feared his eyes, his smile, would melt through the icy barricade I'd erected around my heart, and I needed the frozen barrier to remain. When I thought of Gavin, I only wanted to remember him kissing another woman so I could harbor all of my anger and be strong enough to keep him away.

Mandy suggested talking to him. She said it might bring me closure. But I feared it wouldn't work. Gavin was my weakness. Time away from him had allowed me to see all the ways our relationship had been wrong.

Last Thursday, exactly one week after the "incident," I'd had an especially hard night and decided to make a list comparing my ideal man to Gavin. The outcome surprised me. I wanted a man who would love me wholly. I also wanted a partner whose faith matched my own. Someone who would open my door, hold my hand, pull me into a hug just because. Someone who wanted to share his life with me. When something exciting happened, I wanted to be the first to know. I wanted to be the first to know for the sad things too. And the romantic in me wanted someone who would send me flowers on a random day to let me know I filled his thoughts, not because he was in the doghouse. For discoveries of new food, new movies, crazy adventures—I longed for a companion to share it all with, and Gavin was not that man.

I couldn't fault Gavin on opening my door—he was always a gentleman that way—but I realized things had gotten easy, and I had missed some of the signs. He'd go to church with me when I asked, but whenever I spoke about faith or the Bible, he'd changed the subject. More and more, he had rarely called me. We'd hung out at my suggestion. When I'd asked his opinion, he would smile, shrug, and give some indifferent response.

I decided he sent the roses out of guilt. If he'd wanted to win me back, he would have fought harder. I kicked myself for not realizing sooner. A sense of relief came with this epiphany, and I certainly had no desire to see him.

Rather than go to my regular grocery store, I drove fifteen minutes out of the way to a new strip mall, where a Greenies Grocery was located. A utility truck sat parked across several parking spots. A worker stood in the truck's bucket, raised high above the ground, attaching a Christmas wreath to the light post. I thought about the Christmas gift I had planned to give Gavin—an expensive watch he'd been eyeing for some time. Thankfully, I hadn't bought it yet.

I knew things with Gavin had turned out for the best, but the ache in my heart was slow to subside. It had been a long day, so by the time I arrived at Greenies, I was ready for an all-out round of bumper shopping carts, a game my brother and I had played when we were little.

My mom had hated taking us to the grocery store because we fought over who could push the cart. She had thought if she supplied each of us with our own miniature carts, we would be appeased and she could get her shopping done. She'd miscalculated, by a lot.

Matt and I had fought over who would walk behind Mom, who got to put the cereal in their cart, and who got to unload first. One time I pulled a beautiful maneuver around an old man in an electric cart and squeezed behind Mom before Matt realized what had happened. He was so mad he pulled up beside me and slammed his cart into mine. Of course, I rammed him back, and we realized that the metallic, clashing sound of the carts was oddly invigorating. We collided again and again until Mom lost it. She'd hauled us to the front of the store, strapped us both into the double seat of the huge jumbo cart, and threatened to ground us for a month if we uttered a word. We knew she'd follow through on her threat, so we didn't talk, but we did grin at our new discovery, and it had become a game we'd often repeated.

I completed my shopping, and the only collision was with an unfortunate endcap display of candy-cane air freshener. Thankfully, only two bottles hit the floor.

I exited the store, anxious to get home and eat the rotisserie chicken I'd bought for dinner. Greenies was a happening place. I had parked in a spot at the far end of the lot. I considered the extra sixty seconds it took to walk to the car to be a decent trade-off for the wide-open spaces that surrounded me. I liked not having to worry about scratching someone's door or someone scratching mine. And I liked not feeling lazy.

As I pushed my cart, I growled at the numerous shopping carts left like scattered leaves around the lot. Several carts' front wheels were hooked over the edges of the planters. Some had been abandoned in between parking spots. Was returning a cart really that difficult? I understood the whole caste system and found it depressing that someone's entire job existed solely to compensate for the indolence of society by collecting rogue carts. Greenies provided multiple cart-return areas; in fact, there was one on every aisle. Except, I realized, the one I'd parked on. Figured. But as tempted as I was to forsake my cart to no-man's-land, I would do the ethical thing.

The last bag I loaded into my car was the one with the chicken. The smell of citrus and rosemary made my stomach growl, and I decided to put the bag on the passenger seat in case I needed to taste test it on the way home.

I tossed my purse inside and locked my car so I could trek my cart back to the proper containment unit. The wheels rolled with metallic clatter across the pavement as I crossed from one side of the aisle to the other. Suddenly the sound of the rattling cart was replaced with a roaring engine as the driver of a black truck hauled his vehicle around the corner, then slammed on his brakes, lurching to a stop a mere six feet away from me.

I froze with my cart in hand and glared at the driver. What could be so important that he had turned the grocery store parking lot into the Indy 500? I gritted my teeth and continued toward the other side of aisle, shaking my head at his stupidity.

The driver pulled even with me and matched my pace. I turned to glare again when his hand popped out of his open window, and he waved at me.

"Hey," the guy called. "I'm sorry about that."

"Okay," I replied, looking straight ahead. At least he could admit when he was a jerk.

He drove away, and I shoved my cart into the return rack with a satisfying clang. I pulled my keys from my pocket and walked back to the far end of the lot. When I reached the aisle I needed to cross, déjà vu kicked in. The same black truck rounded the corner again. I clenched my keys in my hand and decided to stand stock-still while the truck drove past. Only it didn't. I rolled my eyes and huffed a deep breath. I wanted my citrus rosemary chicken, not for some guy to use me for target practice. When I looked up to wave the guy through, he smiled at me. A quick scan of the parking lot verified that if this didn't go down well, there were enough people around to hear me scream.

"My name's Jake," he said through his still-open window.

I twisted my lips and looked right at him. He had blond hair, cut short and spiked in front. His eyes were happy, smiling along with his mouth. With his upturned lips and super white teeth, he was a little charming. A little.

"I really am sorry," he said.

"So you said." I crossed my arms and tilted my head. Why was he here?

"I know this is kind of awkward, but can I make it up to you?"

I laughed. "You want to do penance for almost running me over? Volunteer in the PTA, and we'll call it even." My arms fell to my side, and since he had come to a complete stop, I felt it was now safe to cross to my car.

I clicked the doors unlocked, and when I reached for the handle, Jake had the gall to pull into the spot next to me.

He rolled down the passenger window. "Hey, wait a minute," he called.

With a deep breath, I turned around and saw him scramble from his truck. He walked around until he stood right in front of me. He was a few inches taller than my five foot seven, even with the short wedges I wore. I scanned him from head to toe, staring an extra-long minute at his eyes. In the sunlight they were amazing—sincere and comfortable, like a vibrant blue sky.

Jake was handsome. I sucked in my breath and shook my head clear. Being handsome did not give him liberty to drive recklessly around the parking lot . . . unless, of course, his wife was pregnant and had some bizarre craving for ice cream and pickles or his child needed some emergency meds to fight off a raging fever. A quick glance at his left hand showed a ring-free finger, which didn't mean a thing, but I was still glad to see it bare.

When he stood before me at his full height, he was quite impressive, and I lost any advantage I thought I had. I shifted and tried to stand straighter.

He smiled as I raised my eyes back to his face.

"Let me buy you ice cream," he said.

"I've got groceries." I waved my hand toward the car.

"We could meet somewhere in an hour." He shoved his hands into the pockets of his shorts and bounced in his flip-flops like an excited kid. "Or maybe . . . postpone until dinner?" He raised one eyebrow.

"Look, Jake. I appreciate your contrition. You apologized, so let's just call it even." I reached for the door handle.

"I wish I could. But for some reason, I think you doubt my sincerity," he said.

I actually rolled my eyes.

He glanced at his watch. "Do you know where Casa de Taco is?"

"Yeah." My heart pinched. Gavin liked Casa de Taco.

"Okay. I'll be there at six and would love to treat you to dinner and officially prove I *am* sincere. I'd appreciate it if you came and gave me that chance. But . . ." He shrugged his shoulders and offered a tempting smile. "It's up to you. If you've had enough of me and want to continue to wish me dead, you can stand me up and never see me again."

"I can't stand you up. It's not a date." I shifted. "Besides, I haven't agreed to anything."

"Except you are trying to kill me with those looks," he said with a grin.

My frown twisted into a convoluted smile.

"Ah . . . you agree! Do we have a deal?" he asked and bounced again on the balls of his feet.

Was he really excited to pay for my dinner? And if so, why? Was he a stalker or a druggie? Crazy? A loon? Why was I considering saying yes?

"Uh . . . I never got your name," Jake said, raising an expectant eyebrow.

I narrowed my eyes, and my stomach did a little funky fluttery-type thing. Jake may not have been the world's best driver, but he had definitely mastered Flirting 101. My realization should have been a warning, the big, bright neon kind, flashing, *Turn around and run away.* But his easy smile made me want to ignore the warning. If I thought about Jake, I wasn't thinking about Gavin.

"It's Paige," I said.

"Until then, Paige." He walked back to the driver's side of his truck, throwing me another smile before he climbed in. "Six o'clock. Casa de Taco," he called through the open passenger window.

I slid into my car and contemplated the benefits of returning one's shopping cart to the rack. It was always advantageous. Always.

CHAPTER 4

I Ate

MANDY PRACTICALLY SHOVED ME TOWARD my room. "You love Casa de Taco!"

"But I wanted to eat my chicken tonight," I protested. "I'm starving, and I already tortured myself by smelling it all the way home in the car."

Mandy shook her finger at me. "Hmm . . . but you didn't pick at it in the car."

"'Cause I was waiting to share it with you," I said.

"Liar," she said, and I smiled. She continued. "Tell you what. I'll make a delicious pasta salad to go with your chicken for dinner tomorrow, and tonight you can eat with Jake."

I glanced at my phone. "It's already five thirty."

"Then, you'd better hurry." Mandy grabbed my hand, and we ran to raid my closet.

We agreed my favorite jeans and a coral short-sleeved button-up paired with my jean jacket were the perfect combination of relaxed and suave. I didn't touch up my makeup, because that was something I would have done for Gavin, and I didn't want Jake to think he had that kind of power over me. Instead I applied a fresh layer of tinted lip gloss and slipped back into my tan wedges, and Mandy threw me my purse as I hurried out the door.

It wasn't exactly a blind date; it was worse because I didn't know a single person who could vouch for this guy. The only thing I knew about Jake, besides his name, was that he drove like a maniac. Oh, and he was extremely good-looking.

The upside mirrored the downside. While I didn't know a lick about Jake, he didn't know anything about me either. He only knew I was a responsible shopper who returned my cart to the rack. If the night flopped, at least he would rid himself of a guilty conscience and I would get a free meal at Casa de Taco. Mandy would be proud. And those could possibly be the best things that came of my decision to meet Jake.

Dinner with him did offer a clean slate, and that part of the appeal reeled me in. Two weeks of living in the shadow of self-doubt, wondering if Gavin had cheated because of something I had or hadn't done, was exhausting.

And I would get to see Jake's smile a few more times. He had probably wooed lots of ladies with his charming personality, but I was looking for a free dinner, not a boyfriend.

I thought it might do him good to sweat a little, so I purposely waited in the parking lot so I would be five minutes late. Feeling smug, I stepped from my car and then realized what a dork I would look like if he wasn't there. It would be nothing compared to watching front row while Gavin made out with another woman, but a good old cocktail of anxiety and insecurity took hold of my stomach and sent it on a free fall. I moaned and stood on the sidewalk, deliberating which way to go.

My eyes swept the lot to see if anyone stood witness to my neurotic behavior, and I noticed Jake's truck parked in the next aisle over. I took a calming breath and pushed the nausea down. He may still prove to be psychotic, but at least he'd showed up.

With another cleansing breath I hitched my purse up on my shoulder and walked into the restaurant, where the bells tied to the door handle announced my arrival. Jake sat on a long red-vinyl bench next to a couple wrestling three young children. He was easy to spot, as he was easily the hottest thing in the joint. My cheeks warmed at the thought, but I noticed Jake swipe his hands on his jeans as he stood to greet me. Perhaps I wasn't the only one fighting nerves.

"You came," he said, walking toward me and then stopping. He started to lean in for a hug, then switched to a handshake but ended up giving me a conciliatory pat on the arm. Talk about awkward.

I looked him over. He had swapped out his surfer T-shirt and cargo shorts for dark denim and a plaid casual button-down, though he still sported flip-flops. Jake watched me watch him, and my cheeks heated.

"Yes, I'm here," I said lamely.

Jake smiled wider, and a tiny dimple appeared on the left side of his mouth. Some of the awkwardness melted away.

Jake walked to the hostess stand. "My guest has arrived," he said.

"Great," the hostess said with false cheerfulness. She grabbed two menus. "Follow me."

Jake raised his arm and motioned for me to follow the hostess. He seemed to possess some Darcy-esque qualities beyond his handsome features. Casa de Taco did not classify as a classy joint, and this wasn't a date. The restaurant was more in the three-star range, but Jake solidified his man points when he also held my chair.

The hostess tossed my menu at me, then gently opened Jake's before nestling it in his hands and standing by his side for a moment, or two or three, too long. Jake looked up and raised his eyebrows at her. When he didn't utilize his exceptional flirting skills on the ogling high school girl, she frowned. "Your server will be with you shortly," she said as her neck flushed. Then she briskly walked away.

We perused our menus in silence. I read intricate descriptions of burritos and chimichangas and waited for Jake to speak.

He cleared his throat and looked over the top of his menu. "Thanks for coming. I honestly didn't think you'd show." His head tilted slightly to the side. "What made you decide to come?"

Honestly? Had the guy ever looked in the mirror? He had to know how intoxicating his smile was. Who wouldn't want more?

"You seemed pretty repentant," I said with a shrug. "Plus, I don't like to cook."

He laughed, giving me another glimpse of his small dimple, and then he asked, "Well, Paige, what do you like to do?"

"Uh, no." I shook my head. His background check was still incomplete. "You first." I set down my menu. I already knew what I was going to order: a grilled chicken fajita burrito, my regular at Casa de Taco. I propped my elbows on the table and leaned forward with my chin in my hands. "What do *you* like to do, Jake?" I kind of liked this spontaneous me.

"Ok, then." His eyes softened and lit up a bit. "I like to hike, mountain bike, camp, and surf when I get a chance."

"And to make a living? You do make a living, don't you?" I teased.

"I fly," Jake said.

"As in airplanes?"

He nodded.

My, my—he did make a living.

"Who do you fly for?" I asked.

"Uncle Sam," he said with a grin. "I'm stationed at Travis."

That explained the short hair and fit figure. I was pretty sure all military types had to stay in shape. And even if they didn't *have* to, Jake did.

"Isn't Travis almost an hour away? Do you live all the way out here? That's a brutal commute."

"I live near the base, but my parents and sister are here in Grayson. If I time it right, I miss California rush hour," he explained. "I try to get down once a week to help my parents out. That's what I was doing when I"—he forced a fake cough—"ran into you at the store. Making a milk run for my mom."

"The military runs background checks, don't they?" I asked. Perhaps he'd been vetted already.

He clasped his hands on the table and, with a straight face, replied, "Yes, ma'am, they do. If it makes you feel better, I turned twenty-eight in September, I've been granted a top-secret clearance, I have passed all random drug tests, and my mom still calls me sweetie."

It was enough. "Then, I suppose I could forgo the lie detector and fingerprinting," I said with a teasing smile.

The waitress brought water, chips, and salsa. She was friendly and smiled widely at both of us as she took our order. "I'll get that right in," she said and headed for the kitchen.

"I'm embarrassed to admit I don't know anyone in the military," I confessed after the waitress left. "I mean, I know people who know people . . . but that's it." I winced. "Do you think less of me?"

Jake clicked his tongue and shook his head. "No one, huh?"

I felt extremely unpatriotic until he gifted me with his gorgeous smile. The simple action took my breath away, and I grabbed for a drink of my ice water to counteract the flush creeping up my neck.

"Practically everyone I know has a military connection somehow. My dad served too, so it's all I've ever known," Jake said.

"Was he super strict, your dad?" I asked.

Jake laughed. It was a nice sound—warm and welcome. It made me want to smile again, so I did. "Not every military father barks orders at their children," Jake said. "My dad is actually pretty mellow. Most military stereotypes are rumors gone amok. Others are completely accurate."

"What about the cocky fighter pilot?" I asked. "Did Val Kilmer and Tom Cruise get it right?"

Jake flashed his white teeth again. "Yeah, they pretty much nailed it." He leaned forward and whispered secretively, "But I never said I was a fighter pilot. Will you still eat dinner with me?"

Yeah, he was definitely funny. My smile widened, and I agreed to stay for the meal. We fell into easy conversation. It was light and fun and exactly what I needed.

Jake told me about the plane he flew, the C-17 Globemaster. And when he asked, I opened up about my life. Well, mostly. I told him about my master's degree in speech pathology and my work at the middle school. I detailed my family, including my overachieving mother and my adorable niece and nephews. The only hesitation came when he asked about a boyfriend. I dodged the question and ran to the little girl's room. He was wise enough to avoid the topic for the rest of the meal.

He paid for dinner, as promised, and walked me to my car. "So, Paige." His hands found his pockets, and he stared at the ground. I found his insecurity adorable. "I had a nice time tonight. Thanks again for meeting me, and sorry for the whole parking-lot thing. Except if it hadn't happened, I wouldn't be here now." He looked up, and our eyes met.

"Then, I guess, thanks for almost running me over." I paused and inhaled deeply. "And for dinner too."

Uncertainty wedged its way into my lungs, robbing me of air and making my thoughts all confused and jumbled. Dinner had been relaxing, easy. Fun, even. It had been a while since I'd had fun, and I had needed it in a bad way.

Jake raised his hand and wagged his finger between us. "Can we do this again sometime?"

I paused and said a silent prayer. Was it too soon? Was it wrong to say yes? Because I really wanted to say yes. I didn't answer him right away. I fiddled with my purse strap, waiting for a feeling or a thought to indicate this was a bad idea. Nothing negative hit; instead I felt happy, invigorated. "I think I could do that," I said and gave Jake my cell phone number.

"What's your last name, Paige?" he asked as he entered my name and number into his contacts.

"Hall. Yours?"

"Summers."

Jake Summers. I liked the sound of that. I liked him.

"Good night, Captain Summers." I opened my car door and heard Jake's tinkling laugh as I climbed inside. The warm, comfortable sound wrapped around me like a blanket, and I held on to it tightly until I got home, reported to Mandy, climbed into bed, and drifted off to dreamland.

CHAPTER 5
I Waited

AFTER ENJOYING DINNER WITH JAKE, I realized how my relationship with Gavin had drained me. Everything Gavin and I did had revolved around him, and I hadn't even realized it. Gavin's work schedule, Gavin's family commitments, Gavin's workouts, Gavin's restaurant or movie preferences. The list went on and on.

Considering the fact that I had assumed Gavin was the perfect guy, I could admit my instincts weren't reliable, but something with Jake had been great. He was calm, he was easy to be with, and he made me laugh. There was no guarantee he would call, but I hoped he would. So I waited.

Mandy had received the play-by-play when I'd gotten home from dinner, but the next day during our lunch break in the staff room, she wanted more. "I feel lucky if I get good coupons at the grocery store, yet you have a complete stranger run you over, and look what happens," she said while she scooped up a spoonful of yogurt.

"I wouldn't call him a complete stranger. Not anymore," I teased from my position in front of the copy machine.

"Wow, Paige. This is so unlike you. I mean, you haven't been spontaneous since before . . ." Her voice dropped off, but I knew what she was going to say.

"I know. I had the same thought over and over this morning." I grabbed my copies from the dispenser and walked to where Mandy sat. "I think that's part of what made it so great. Plus, he's pretty dreamy."

The shrill bell marked the end of lunch. Mandy moaned as she dumped her trash into the bin, and then she left for her room. Mandy taught science and was a newbie like me. We were both teaching for our third year at the school but still considered ourselves rookies compared to the old-timers we had on site.

At our first staff meeting, the principal had encouraged us to embrace technology. She'd suggested several ways we could incorporate it in class, much to the dismay of the older generation. Completing an online grade-book capped their tech abilities. But Mandy had jumped right on board with the principal and suggested ways the kids could use their smartphones in class. Senior staff members grumbled, but the principal loved Mandy's input.

Rather than ostracize herself from the rest of the staff, Mandy had offered to teach a tech class to any interested teachers after school on Mondays and asked if I would help. Her enthusiasm was contagious, and after the first class, where we demonstrated how to link websites to the teacher pages, Mandy had become a hit.

I'd helped her during tech class by walking around and individually assisting those who were stumped. Eventually, I'd taught a few of the ses-sions, covering the gradebook program and some smartphone apps I'd found useful for sending students reminders about assignments, due dates, and announcements. When the principal had nominated Mandy for teacher of the year, she'd refused to accept unless she could share the honor with me.

Two months later we were roommates. We'd found a modest-sized rental home and grown as close as sisters. We shared dish duty, swapped stories about students, and cried collectively over bad dates and good boyfriends. We'd shed happy tears when Mandy's boyfriend, Brandon, proposed a few months ago. Mandy was fabulous, and it was a plus she shared my love of all things Jane Austen.

After my last student exited the classroom, Mandy's dark-haired head poked through the doorway as though my thoughts had summoned her. "I have a fabulous idea," she gushed and walked to where I stood restacking the word-blend blocks I used as learning manipulatives.

"Yeah?" I stopped and looked up at her.

"Invite him to the career fair," Mandy said with far too much glee.

"Who?" I asked, then realized. "Jake?"

"Yeah. The air force is always looking for new recruits. Haven't you seen the billboards?"

The thought of him made my stomach tingle. I smiled but shook my head and went back to my task.

"Tell me you haven't been thinking about him all day," Mandy said. I refused to answer. Of course I had. "It's the perfect chance to see him again," she said. "Call him and make up some story about each teacher needing to find a volunteer, and ask if he can come."

"It's a month away," I pointed out and sank into a nearby chair.

Mandy shrugged. "But it's golden."

I planted my chin in my palm. "It would be golden if I had his number, which I don't." Why hadn't I asked for it again? Oh yeah—I hadn't wanted to appear clingy or too interested. I wasn't looking for a relationship. Lame.

Mandy moaned. "I wish he would call already!"

"Mandy," I said, "I can't do this." I stood up and began erasing my whiteboard. "Everything with Gavin is too fresh. I can't get caught up with another guy I barely know. I can't sit by the phone, pining away. I'm done wasting heartbeats on undeserving men." I turned to face her.

"Is that an Austen line?" she asked, and I shook my head no. "Well, it should be."

"Look, if he calls, he calls," I said.

"Flyboy will call," Mandy said with a wink, and I threw my eraser at her as she slipped out the door.

Everything I had told Mandy was the truth, no matter how much I hoped Jake proved me wrong.

Either way, I kept my phone fully charged.

After three days of phone silence, I cracked. Thoughts of Gavin were diminishing, but only because I'd replaced them with thoughts of Jake. I tried to keep Gavin away by swapping him out, and it made no sense. How could a guy I'd seen for two hours replace ten months of a relationship? Jake was not the rebound guy. And since he hadn't called, he wasn't any sort of guy beyond the one who'd almost run me over and then taken me to dinner to apologize.

After six days, it had been long enough for me to resign myself to the fact that he wasn't going to call. I could now claim I had once met someone in the military who flew airplanes and that we'd enjoyed a nice dinner.

I went to church with my family and decided to go home for a few hours before heading over to Mom and Dad's house later for dinner. I got home, kicked off my heels, and tossed my purse onto the table. Seconds later my phone started ringing.

"Hi, Paige. This is Jake Summers," he said, and my heart melted like gooey chocolate at the sound of his voice.

"General Summers. How have you been?" I asked, rather proud of the fact that my voice didn't crack.

He laughed at my advancement of rank. Google had provided some air force facts, as well as some about Travis Air Force Base and the Globemaster. I wasn't obsessed; I'd had a lot of time on my hands, and Google had practically begged to be used.

"Actually, you were correct the other day. I'm a captain," he said.

"Captain, huh? I thought captains sailed on ships." Maybe Google hadn't been too helpful.

"They fly planes too. Pretty much any type of transportation," he explained.

"What about a motorcycle?" I asked.

"You've seen *Top Gun*. What do you think?"

"I think Maverick rocks a motorcycle. Was he a captain?" I enjoyed our playful banter. It was easy, noncommittal.

"Nah, he was in the navy. Their ranking is different." There was a pause on the line. "Hey, sorry I couldn't call sooner," Jake said. "I've been out of town."

I collapsed onto my couch in a clump of contentment.

"You didn't have to call at all." I took a breath and said, "But I'm glad you did."

"I like to keep my word," Jake said simply, and I fell silent.

Jake had said exactly what I'd needed to hear. He kept his word, which was the polar opposite of Gavin, who said beautiful things and offered hollow guarantees. I'd listened to Gavin. I'd believed him. Yet, in the end, I wasn't worth the required effort. He'd claimed he loved me, but it wasn't enough to commit to me. It wasn't love at all.

Jake had said he would call, and he did. It wasn't much to go on, but for now, it was enough.

After a minute, Jake asked, "Paige? You okay?"

I answered him with a soft laugh. "Yeah," I said. "So tell me about your trip."

And he did. He explained he had a crazy-unpredictable schedule. His plane supported missions in the United States and all throughout the Pacific. He told me the main purpose was to transport troops or supplies to various locations, which meant he made frequent short trips to drop stuff off or pick it up and head back home. Sometimes he would be gone for a few days, and other times he was gone for a few weeks, particularly if the assignment was to fly to Asia or if there was a training exercise.

Bummer, I thought. But instead I said, "Wow. It sounds like a pretty cool plane."

"It's one of the newest airframes," he said. I could hear the enthusiasm in his voice. "It has a glass cockpit—"

"What does that even mean?" I asked. "Don't all airplanes have glass in the cockpit?"

Jake laughed.

I smiled.

"I have an idea," he said. "Why don't I show you?"

"Show me?" I repeated like an idiot.

My phone beeped with another call. A quick glance showed my mom's profile.

"Yeah, I'll give you a personal tour of the base," Jake said, and I sent my mom to voicemail.

My stomach tumbled again. Conflicting emotions—fear of moving too fast and fear of being dormant—clashed beneath my ribs.

"What do you say? Do you have a day you could come up?" Jake asked.

"Um, I work all week . . ." My phone buzzed again. Geesh, couldn't Mom take a hint?

"Then, how about Saturday?" He sounded excited, and I could picture him bouncing in his shoes like he had the day we'd met in the Greenies parking lot.

"Saturday works," I said. "What time?"

"Let's meet at the west gate at noon. I'll take you to lunch and show you around." Jake's voice was happy.

"I'm looking forward to it," I said.

I hung up the phone and wondered for a minute if I was doing the right thing. Then I realized I was tired of worrying. Accepting Jake's invitation made me as happy as he sounded, and he seemed genuine. No one would get hurt. No one would be put out. And both parties would be mutually content. I smiled. Seeing Jake again would be the best thing to happen all week, and I couldn't wait.

CHAPTER 6
I Imploded

THE MOMENT I WALKED INTO my childhood home, the questions began. "Why didn't you answer my calls? Were you on the phone? Who were you talking to?" My mother was not subtle, and I thought my head might implode.

"Mom, you can't just expect me to drop everything when you call," I said. "You sat next to me at church, and you knew I was coming for dinner." I tossed my purse onto a chair and set the salad I'd brought on the counter.

"But I needed you to bring a teaspoon of chili powder. I ran out, and that's why I kept calling. Since you didn't answer, I had to improvise. I hope the enchiladas turn out, because the chili powder really makes a difference." She picked a piece of ground beef from the pan and popped it into her mouth. "Mmm, I don't know."

I leaned over and gave her a kiss on the cheek. "They'll be great, Mom. You could make turnips, and they would taste amazing."

My mother smiled triumphantly. I often chastised her for being overbearing and overprotective, but she was fabulous in the kitchen. A trait I definitely did not inherit.

"Well?" she said and let the question dangle.

"Well, what?" I snatched some cheese from her grated pile.

She swatted my hand. "Why didn't you answer?" she persisted. I narrowed my eyes and gave her a look meant to shame her. Instead she perked up her eyebrows and rinsed her hands in the sink. "What? I want to make sure you're doing okay. Is that a crime?"

I sighed and resigned myself to the fact that she would find out sooner or later. "I was talking to someone." I plopped into a chair at the bar and watched her wash dishes.

"Who?" she asked, keeping her tone light in an attempt to make the interrogation seem natural. She failed miserably.

"A guy I met," I said.

The water immediately shut off, and Mom leaned across the counter, eager for more. "When?"

"Last Monday. His name is Jake Summers," I began.

"Whose name?" Dad said. He slipped his shoes off outside the sliding door and joined Mom and me in our powwow at the counter.

"A guy Paige met," Mom said, grinning widely.

"Where did you meet him?" Dad asked.

"Uh . . . at the grocery store," I hedged, and it sounded more like a question than a statement.

"And you gave him your number?" Mom looked scandalized.

"Well, we went out to eat, and then I gave him my number." The scrutiny was suffocating, but truth was truth. I walked to the cupboard and took out a glass. I could hear Mom and Dad whispering behind me. After filling my cup, I turned back toward them. "Look, can you hold your horses until everyone else gets here? Then I can tell you all at once what happened."

"Okay," Dad said with a shrug.

"Fine," Mom agreed. But her lips pinched into a thick line, and I could tell she wasn't fine. "You've waited this long to tell us. It's not like another thirty minutes matters now." Great. I'd hurt her feelings.

I hated this pattern we constantly cycled through. Mom was nosy and wanted to know details—all the details. I was twenty-five, almost twenty-six, and while I enjoyed being pampered by my mother, she wouldn't acknowledge that I could put sheets on a bed without her walking me through the steps. She tried to hold my hand for everything. It used to not be a big deal. I figured she could teach me a thing or two. But I also figured once I graduated, moved out, and had my own life, things would change. She would recognize I could be independent. I knew how to balance a checkbook, pump a tank of gas, and reheat leftovers. I figured wrong. Mom still called and constantly nitpicked and questioned any and every decision I made.

That's how the spiral always began. Then came the downward slide where I would push her away, ignore her calls, or explain with blunt force that I was an independent adult. Mom would retreat, make comments with subliminal messages, and the guilt would begin to creep in. Next came the step where I trudged through mounds of remorse trying to make her feel better.

It was so unfair. I hadn't done anything wrong except live, yet my conscience felt heavy and guilt-ridden. Mom wasn't doing anything wrong either. She was looking out for me, the way she knew how. Granted, she was a hovering parent. The kind with giant swooping helicopter blades, overshadowing everything I did or said. Mom would classify as the type with double propellers. She could cut me up any direction I moved. I'd have to ask Jake what those were called.

Heather, Greg, their three kids, and Matt showed up at six thirty, and one bite into the enchiladas, Mom's questions erupted. "So, Paige, you were going to tell us about Jake."

"Jake?" Matt said with shifting intonation.

So I told them about meeting Jake at the grocery store, without disclosing the reckless driving and near-death experience. I focused on the part where he'd approached me and asked me to meet him for dinner.

"And you did it? Way to go, girl!" Heather leaned across the table and gave me a fist bump.

"Me too." Amelia held her fist out, and Matt gave her a gentle bump on her knuckles, then opened his fingers while making explosion noises. Max screamed and mimicked Amelia's motion, so Matt offered him a fist bump as well. He was a good uncle.

Mom shifted in her seat. "He could have kidnapped you," she said with a condescending tone and exaggerated frown.

"I figured meeting in public at a restaurant was pretty safe," I defended myself. "Besides, he's in the military, and he turned out to be really nice."

"Oh, a man in uniform," Heather teased. "Good job, Paige."

"He was polite, and he's a pilot at Travis," I added.

"There's a guy in my physics study group who's in the ROTC program. He told me he got a pilot slot, but he's heard training is pretty hard. I guess a lot of guys wash out," Matt said.

Jake hadn't. Another plus for him. I took a bite.

"Well, good for you, honey," Dad said. "I'm glad you had a nice time instead of sitting home moping over Ga—"

Greg pretended to choke. Heather beat him on the back while trying to contain her huge smile. Nathanial was lying on a blanket next to Heather's chair. He started to fuss, so she picked him up and moved him to her lap.

I laughed. "It's good. I'm good," I assured my family. "I'm going to meet Jake at the base on Saturday, and he's going to show me around." I raised my hand to preempt any questions. "He's got a security clearance, and I'm sure there are guys with guns all over the place. It will be fine."

"A security clearance doesn't guarantee he's not a slimeball. Gavin's proof that looks can be deceiving," Mom said.

"I totally agree with you. But this is only for lunch and a quick tour," I said.

"I'm happy for you," Heather said, and with the exception of a dozen sideways glances, Amelia and Max led the conversation for the rest of the meal.

Jake texted on Thursday. *Are we still on for Saturday?*

I analyzed the fact that he capitalized and used proper punctuation for way too long and wondered if I would appear desperate or efficient if I texted him back right away. I was my mother's daughter. The details killed me.

I waited an hour and texted back, *Yep, see you at noon. West gate, right?*

His reply came back immediately. *Yes, west gate. I can't wait.*

I didn't respond, but Friday passed slower than a snail on diazepam.

Saturday morning Mandy left with her brother to visit their grandpa for the day. I needed a second opinion, so I took lots of selfies and sent them to Heather to approve my outfit.

We decided on a pair of fitted jeans and a flower-print crepe shirt layered over a white camisole and under a three-quarter-length-sleeve pink cardigan. Silver wedge sandals and minimal makeup completed the look. After a pep talk from Heather about why it was great for me to get out again, I gave myself a quick glance in the mirror, then climbed into my car for the hour-long drive.

When I was about halfway to the military base, Jake called. The butter-flies in my stomach got a sudden sugar rush, and I answered through my Bluetooth.

"Paige." The way he said my name, I knew something was wrong. The butterflies dive-bombed my gut. "You're gonna hate me," he said.

Hate may have been a bit extreme. I didn't respond, and I could hear the hesitation as Jake continued. "I have to cancel. I was called in on alert and have to take off on a trip. I leave in an hour," he said.

I gripped the steering wheel tightly and bit the inside of my cheek, concentrating on the pain in my mouth rather than the humiliation I felt at having jumped to the conclusion that Jake actually wanted to see me.

"Paige?" He said only my name, but he sounded sincere. It made me angry.

"I'm just looking for a place to turn around," I said bluntly.

Jake groaned. "I'm so sorry. We have to sit these alerts all the time, but I've only been called in once before. I honestly didn't think it would be a problem. Say you're not angry?"

I let out a single laugh in response.

Jake sighed into the phone. "Okay, that was a dumb thing to say. Of course you're angry. Please, let me make it up to you."

"Where are you going?" I asked.

Jake hesitated. "I . . . I can't tell you."

"Of course. It's top secret," I said lightly.

Through the silence I heard a female voice call his name. "Jake, we've gotta start the brief," she said.

I pulled off the freeway into a residential area. "It sounds like you're needed," I said.

This time he was silent. I turned onto a side street, parked, and then shut my eyes. Maybe if I pressed my eyelids closed hard enough, I could keep my emotions at bay. There was no way Jake could know he had this effect on me. *Why* did he have this effect on me?

When he spoke again, his voice was low, resigned. "I was really looking forward to seeing you again, and now I'm afraid I've messed it all up."

Oh, how I wanted to believe him, but the fissures in my heart had not healed enough to trust. Gavin had definitely messed me up. "Fly safe, okay?" I said, and then I hung up.

CHAPTER 7
I Moped

I RETURNED HOME, AND THAT night I repeated the story three times for Mandy while she analyzed it from every possible angle. Detailed conversational scrutiny must be a girl thing. She tried to convince me it was no big deal, but her smile didn't reach her eyes, and I knew she was just as confused with Jake's behavior as I was. It wouldn't have been such a big deal if he'd told me beforehand that he would possibly be called in to work, but the way it had gone down felt like a punch to the gut. The best Mandy could do was repeat the fact that Jake didn't know how Gavin had hurt me. He didn't know how hard it had been for me to jump in and trust him. Mandy tried to convince me Jake would make up for it when he got home, but her arguments sounded like she was trying to convince herself, too.

"Let's see what he does when he gets back before we pass judgment," she told me again.

"I'll consider it," I said. "Hey, will you start this?" I tossed her my DVD copy of *Sense and Sensibility*. "I'll make the cocoa." Marianne's whining was a measly substitute for Jake, but Mandy did point out that the movie I'd selected included a military man. She claimed the fact that Colonel Brandon fought for his ladylove had to be a good sign.

When I woke up Sunday morning, my head still ached, so I missed church and slept for the majority of the day. While I knew my reaction was immature, I called Mom and told her my head throbbed and I wouldn't make it to Sunday dinner. I didn't want my family to read my emotions, I didn't want them to see me moping, and I didn't want to answer any questions about Jake. I couldn't have answered their questions anyway, so it was easier to avoid them. I was pleasantly surprised when Mom accepted my excuse without a litany of questions. She simply suggested I take meds and go to bed.

The next few days passed as normal, which meant they were filled with boring, routine kinds of stuff. I enjoyed working with my students, but after work I wasted hours on the internet watching videos of stupid animal tricks.

Was this the reality of my life? Did boredom always loom around me? Because I despised it. Maybe one of the reasons I'd stayed with Gavin was because I needed someone or something to occupy my time. But I thought we'd been happy, in love.

I decided to be done with memes and work on my cooking. Lasagna sounded like a great place to start. I put my Google skills to use and found a highly rated recipe for vegetarian lasagna. I was even creative enough to substitute lettuce for spinach, because who really liked spinach anyway? Besides, they were the same color, had the same leafy look, and were from the same food family—whatever.

The doorbell rang right after I slid the pan into the oven. I grinned at my accomplishment and wiped my hands on the dish towel before answering the door.

A lanky high-school-aged boy stood on the mat, holding a bouquet. "Are you Ms. Hall?" he asked, and the huge arrangement almost toppled when the boy shifted.

I pulled the door open wider. "Yes, you can set those right here." I motioned to the coffee table, and my grin grew. Jake was well on his way to making up for last Saturday. "Let me grab my purse," I said, figuring I should tip the poor kid.

"The tip's already been covered," he said.

"Are you sure?" I asked. After waiting tables in college, I hated stiffing anyone who worked for tips.

The kid raised his brows and smiled. "Yeah, I'm sure. He was pretty generous."

Jake's status notched up a bit more. I shut the door behind the delivery guy and walked a slow circle around the huge bouquet now sitting on my living room coffee table. The flowers could not have been more perfect: white daisies, red gerberas, and half a dozen yellow gladioli. I leaned over the flowers and inhaled with my eyes closed. When I opened them again, I noticed the card and plucked it from the plastic triton before flopping down onto the couch to read:

My feelings have not changed, and I hope you will forgive me.
Please talk to me? I miss you. —Gavin

My lungs depleted, and my mind suddenly felt like it had been stuffed with a giant wad of fuzzy cotton candy. I clamped my eyes shut and pressed the heels of my hands to my temples.

Gavin? Gavin sent the flowers—not Jake? The elation from only moments before evaporated, and I growled in frustration.

Mandy walked through the door, her arms loaded with papers she quickly dropped onto the kitchen table. Her eyes turned first to the bouquet, then to me. "I told you," she said.

I rolled my eyes. "Yeah, you told me Jake would make up for Saturday, not that Gavin would ask me to"—I made air quotes—"*talk to him.*"

Mandy's mouth fell open. Without looking behind her, she dropped her purse beside her piles on the table. "Those are from Gavin?"

I scrunched my nose and nodded. "I should have known they weren't from Jake. That would be too good to be true, and my mom would be the first to remind me that if it seems too good to be true, it probably is." I leaned my head against the back of the couch. "I thought they were from him," I whined.

Mandy walked over and sat next to me on the couch. I handed her the card, and after glancing it over, she said, "I'm sorry."

I lifted my head back up to look at her again. "What was I thinking? Jake couldn't send flowers 'cause he has no idea where I live. I'm such an idiot." I pulled my hair over my left shoulder and ran my fingers through the strands. "Dumb boys," I said and pursed my lips into a frown.

"Don't give up yet, Paige," Mandy said. "You'll find Mr. Right." She handed the card back to me.

I scoffed and tossed it onto the coffee table. Mandy was living proof that fairy-tale endings exist. With her princess-cut engagement ring hugging her delicate finger, she leaned over and smelled the flowers. Mandy had been taking night classes to get her master's when she met Brandon on campus. They had dated for three months, and before Brandon left for his internship in Irvine, he'd proposed. Mandy had stayed in Central California, Brandon temporarily lived in Southern California, and the wedding was four months away, during spring break.

"When will I get to meet my Mr. Right?" I said.

"Maybe you already have." Mandy stood and gathered all of her stuff from the table.

"Grading?" I asked.

She nodded and walked down the hall to her room.

I leaned forward and pulled one of the gerbera daisies from the vase. Twirling it in my fingers, I watched the thin petals spin around and around. It was the perfect analogy for my love life—twirling and twirling but never landing on anything solid or concrete. I didn't need a whirlwind romance like Mandy. I had been the model of patience when it came to Gavin, never pushing too far or too much. I'd never made demands or set ultimatums. Maybe I'd made it too easy for him. Maybe if I had pushed, he would know he couldn't mess around and then just ask me to forgive him. But I didn't want a man to love me because I pushed him. I wanted a man to not cheat because he loved me too much to consider it. I wanted loving me to be enough.

Mandy walked back into the living room and sniffed the air. "What's that smell?" she asked.

"Oh no! I forgot about my lasagna," I said as I jumped off the couch and hurried to the kitchen. I quickly opened the oven door, pulled the pan out of the heat, and set it atop the stove.

Mandy watched me with large eyes. "You cooked?" she asked.

With a large spoon I poked at the pan and ignored her.

"You hate cooking," she said.

I retrieved a knife and a spatula. "Only because I'm not very good at it." I began edging the knife around the outside of the pan. After I cleared the perimeter, I cut down a row and then divided it into three pieces. Setting the knife aside, I grabbed two plates while I answered Mandy. "This recipe looked easy, and I was bored. It smells great." I inhaled the bubbly mozzarella, and my glass of optimism returned to half-full.

Mandy lowered one eyebrow and watched me maneuver the spatula under my perfectly square piece. I bit my lower lip while I slowly lifted the lasagna to my plate and then served Mandy. The spatula dropped with a satisfying clink on the glass pan, and I carried both plates to the table.

After one more trip for napkins and forks, I cut through the gooey cheese and took my first bite. My glass quickly drained from half full to empty. Wandering-through-a-hot-desert-for-days-without-water kind of empty. The lasagna tasted like wet leaves.

"Is this lettuce?" Mandy asked. I looked up to see a withered clump of romaine hanging from Mandy's fork.

I nodded mutely.

"Paige, why would you put lettuce in lasagna?"

"It was vegetarian, and I didn't want to add spinach," I explained. "They're both leafy plants."

"You can't substitute lettuce for spinach." She grimaced and flicked the slimy leaf onto her plate.

My moment of triumph disappeared, and I slowly sagged in my seat, deflating as quickly as a giant bouncy house once the air is turned off.

Mandy sighed. "Let me take you to dinner."

"No. I can't waste all this food." I waved my hand over my plate. "There are starving kids who would love to have this lasagna even though it's all screwed up." I forced another bite into my mouth.

"You're really gonna eat it?" Mandy asked and scrunched up her nose.

I nodded while I chewed.

Mandy picked up her purse and keys. "Fine. I'm going to Millie's for a BLT and custard, and when I get back, we're going to discuss what to do about Gavin and those stupid, beautiful flowers."

I whimpered, and she walked out the door.

CHAPTER 8
I Waffled

MANDY AND I AGREED THAT talking with Gavin might help bring closure. The part we couldn't agree on was whether the talk should be in person or over the phone. We asked my sister, who voted for in person so there would be nothing left to speculate about. I could tell Gavin he'd thrown away any chance we'd had and there would be no reconciling. Yet, every time I picked up my phone to call him, I waffled. His picture pulled up with his name, a candid I had shot while he was laughing at something someone had said. It captured everything I loved about him: his humor, his gorgeous eyes, his easygoing mood when he let his guard down. It was a great picture.

After two days of my putting it off, Gavin texted me. *Did you like the flowers?*

Me: *They were beautiful—thanks.*

Gavin: *And?*

Me: *Millie's, Tuesday @ 4:30?*

Gavin: *I'll be there.*

I didn't mean for our talk to be a test of Gavin's contrition, but it would be. More than four weeks had passed since I witnessed his indiscretion, and I had thought about it at least once a day, usually more. I'd chosen the late afternoon to meet because I wanted to avoid the dinner crowd, but Gavin never got off early. He would have to sacrifice some precious work time to meet me, and it hit me that I'd rarely asked him to sacrifice anything for our relationship. I had often changed plans, adjusted my schedule, and sacrificed over and over to meet his needs because I'd thought it would make him happy. Making him happy was all I had wanted.

I dressed especially cute for work and replayed the memory of Gavin and the brunette over and over throughout the day so I would be freshly irate by the time we met.

Miranda complimented my outfit, then asked, "Do you have a date with Gavin after work?"

I reveled in the renewed anger I'd been brewing throughout the day and smiled wickedly. "Actually, I am meeting Gavin. I haven't spoken with him since I caught him kissing another woman. It should be fun." She looked effectively shocked. Poor Miranda. I'd have to apologize for my sarcasm later.

While I expected Gavin to be on time, I didn't feel the need to impress him anymore, so although my punctuality had me parked at the curb by 4:20, I sat in my car and watched Gavin walk in and fidget nervously until 4:35. But waiting any longer only procrastinated the inevitable, so I got out and joined him inside Millie's.

He leaned forward to kiss my cheek, but I halted him with my hand on his chest. He smiled sadly, looked me over, and said, "You look great, Paige. You always do."

His compliment touched me more than it should, on top of the fact that he looked rather delicious himself. He wore his charcoal suit, the one he knew was my favorite, and I figured we were playing the same game. My thoughts betrayed me for a minute as I reverted to my old self and wondered how I had lucked out to get such a handsome guy to notice me. I knew I wouldn't be able to push away everything I'd felt for him, which was why I hadn't wanted to see him before. But today I'd let the anger boil inside, and it had thickened into a draft of culpability and regret. Gavin had cheated. I'd suffered because of that choice. In the end, I figured, we'd both lost, but in reality, perhaps only I had. Either way, I refused to be swayed by his smile.

Gavin led me to a table, and we skimmed the polite topics of work and family until the waitress took our orders.

Once she walked away, I began. "So?"

"So . . ." Gavin repeated. He reached for my hands on the table, but I quickly pulled them to my lap. He sighed sadly. "Paige, I'm so sorry. Those words can't even begin to describe how I feel, but I don't know what else to say."

"You told me you were busy," I said, picturing the scene again.

Gavin ran a hand through his hair. His vulnerability revealed a disturbingly attractive side of him. I always had liked him best when he let his guard down.

"I know. I didn't mean for it to happen." His hands returned to the table, and he folded them neatly and leaned toward me.

"Who was she?" I'd thought about this over and over and had decided it didn't matter, but curiosity won out.

Gavin lowered his eyes and resigned himself to answering. "Her name's Molly. She's on my sales team. We wanted to celebrate the new account—"

I cut him off. "I wanted to celebrate with you, remember?"

He sighed. "I didn't see your text until later. A bunch of the team was supposed to come, but they all bailed, and then it was just the two of us. One thing led to another . . ."

"Yeah, I saw that particular part," I said.

The waitress delivered Gavin's club sandwich and my clam chowder, then retreated quickly. Tension oozed from our table.

"How did you . . . ? I mean, I didn't . . ." Gavin sighed. "I wish I could take it back," he said.

Gavin never failed to find the right words. Eloquence dripped from his lips like golden honey. To see him tongue-tied both humbled and bolstered me. A little part of me hurt because I knew he was hurting. But the majority of me realized that while his words were genuine, and his feelings were probably genuine too, he and I would never work. Whatever bridge had connected us before was now damaged beyond repair.

"Thank you for telling me. I want you to know I didn't doubt you. Not for a minute. I came over to surprise you with dinner so *we* could celebrate," I said, pointing between the two of us.

"I told Molly nothing could happen between us. I told her it was a mistake. She's already transferred to another team." Gavin looked up and pleaded with his beautiful eyes. "Could you ever forgive me, Paige? Is there any chance we could try again?"

The moment held taut, and I wondered how he could consider the possibility of a future between us. I could forgive him for eating the last chocolate truffle, the one I'd been saving all week, or for forgetting to buy stamps and then commandeering all of mine. I could even forgive him for not buying sparklers on the Fourth of July despite the fact that I'd told him how much I love sparklers. But cheating? Kissing another woman? I knew I would eventually forgive him, but I would never again trust him, which meant there was no reason to try again.

"No," I said and swallowed past the lump in my throat. Despite the barrier of anger I'd built around my heart, I hurt. "I can't. I'm sorry."

Gavin nodded slowly, then dropped his eyes to stare blankly at his plate of food. I tried to take a few bites of chowder, but it tasted like chalk on my tongue, so I dropped my spoon to my bowl.

We sat silently for a minute more, until I suggested we leave. I hated wasting the food, but I needed to get away before I suffocated.

Gavin held the door for me, and we walked outside. "Can I still call you?" he asked.

I shook my head. "I need time to forget about you." The sadness in my heart stifled my attempted smile.

"I don't want you to forget." Gavin reached out and fingered the end of my hair. "At least don't forget the good times," he added. "I am sorry I hurt you, Paige. I hope you find happiness." Gavin moved his hand to my arm. He leaned in again, and this time I let him kiss my cheek as a final goodbye.

As much as I loved Millie's Café, I walked away thinking I enjoyed dinner at Casa de Taco a whole lot more.

CHAPTER 9
I Simplified

I FINISHED OUT THE WEEK at school and kept busy helping Mandy with wedding plans. She wanted a simple ceremony, and after watching my mom and sister plan their version of perfection for Heather's wedding, I agreed with the route Mandy and Brandon were taking. Simplicity. All that mattered at the end of the day was that they were married. Would a deejay, expensive catering, or a five-tier cake matter? Heather had made a huge fuss about how things had to be, and then she'd spent the entire day staring into Greg's eyes. It was enchanting and extremely frustrating, because while Heather ended up not caring, Mom had still made Matt and me run around to twist all the twinkle lights outward so they could project to maximum effect.

I decided to adopt the slogan of simplicity. By definition, simplicity meant I would cut back rather than add more to my life. I'd always thought living life to the fullest meant filling my days with a variety of things, but maybe the reality was if I cut back, I could better enjoy the activities I selected to do.

The second half of my new philosophy included a pledge to embrace spontaneity. If I wanted to cook, I would. And when I didn't want to, I wouldn't. If I saw a cute guy, I would talk to him. I would go on last-minute dates, work out when I wanted, and talk to my mom on my terms.

There were two times when I would not settle for simplicity and spontaneity: when it came to God and when it came to my students. My faith would remain my priority. My prayers and worship would continue. And I would lesson-plan and work diligently on my students' behalf.

The new week marked a new beginning for me. I walked into work with my head high. I wanted to exude confidence, but I also wore a great pair of heels I'd found while out shopping with Mandy. I normally didn't wear something so flashy to work, but I liked the bright-yellow peep toes. I'd matched them with gray dress pants and a floral wrap shirt with matching yellow flowers. Spontaneity trailed in my wake.

My morning was filled with parent meetings to update families on their students' progress and set new goals. In between my appointments, Miranda stuck her head around the corner of my door. "More flowers, Miss Hall," she said hesitantly.

She walked in carrying another large arrangement, this one made entirely of stargazer lilies. The heavenly fragrance reached my desk before Miranda did.

"I guess your boyfriend isn't letting you go without a fight." She gave a timid smile. And who could blame her? I'd lashed out unnecessarily the last time she tried to talk to me about romance.

I still felt bad about that, so I smiled and then sighed. "I honestly don't know why he'd send these after our conversation last week."

"You may not like him anymore, but he's got great taste in flowers." She set the vase on a nearby worktable. "I wish my husband would think to send me flowers outside of our anniversary." She turned the vase, inhaled, and sighed.

"They are beautiful. Thanks, Miranda." I offered a genuine smile, and she left the room.

Acting on my new spontaneity mantra, I picked up my phone and texted Gavin. *Why did you send more flowers?*

Perhaps I should have said thank you. The flowing pink-and-white petals with speckled centers were the most gorgeous flowers I'd ever received, but I needed to let go of all things Gavin.

I began my final appointment with a single mom. Afterward I had two sets of students left for the day. Gavin didn't respond for almost thirty minutes. I heard my phone vibrate but finished my appointment before checking the message.

His response didn't make any sense. *???—I wanted to meet with you.*

Me: *I thought I was pretty clear at Millie's. I need to move on.*

Gavin: *You were extremely clear then, but I'm confused now.*

Me: *You didn't send me flowers today? Lilies?*

His response was delayed, but he finally replied. *No, but if you like them, I'll take the credit.*

The moment froze. I stood in front of my desk, phone in hand, feeling like I was in a dream. I saw my reaction, as if from afar—my jaw slack in confusion, my eyes wide—and at the same time, my heart sped.

The next bell rang, and I instantly zoomed back to reality. Four of my six students entered the room.

"Go ahead and pull your work from your files," I said automatically.

The kids turned to their task, and I scanned the bouquet, looking for a card. The remaining two students came in chatting, and I quickly directed them to grab their files and move to their workstations.

I couldn't find a card, and my temper flared. Gavin was playing with me. He had to have sent the flowers in an attempt to subliminally make me think of him. What galled me more was that his plan had worked. Once I saw the bouquet, my thoughts had immediately turned in his direction.

Me: *I have to teach. Please stop sending flowers.*

I tossed my phone into my purse and sat down to review word blends with my students. My phone vibrated a few minutes later. I ignored it for an entire five minutes before curiosity got the best of me. I put the students into groups and gave them two minutes to complete a word-building exercise.

Gavin: *I took you at your word. The flowers are not from me, but I hope they make you smile. I miss your smile, and you deserve only the best.*

My frustration deflated like a slow leak from a helium balloon. Guilt for being rude to Gavin settled in my gut. I debated whether or not I should text him back but decided to wait and talk to Mandy. My mind was in too much of a whirl. Besides making contact with Gavin, I had falsely accused him. Now I still had no notion who the flowers were from.

I inhaled deeply and refocused on my students. My spontaneity for texting Gavin hadn't worked out very well, so I reverted to simplicity and told myself to focus on the here and now. Focus on my students. Focus on getting through the next two hours so Mandy could help me solve the mystery of the lilies.

When the final bell rang, I proudly walked my kids to the door and watched them until they turned the corner at the end of the hall. Then I took slow, deliberate steps back toward my desk. The rich scent of the lilies hit my nose, and I bit my lip as I scoured the arrangement again, looking for any indication of their sender. As I tilted the vase onto its side to look on the bottom, Mandy walked in.

"My, my, you lucky girl. More flowers, huh?" She walked over to me and inhaled deeply. "Wow! Those are amazing."

No secret clues were etched into the vase, so I set the flowers upright. "I thought Gavin sent them, but I texted him, and he swore it wasn't him. I have no idea who they're from," I said.

"But someone delivered them?" Mandy fingered one of the elongated petals.

"Yeah," I said with a sigh of frustration. "Miranda brought them in after my lunch appointment."

"Have you asked her?" Mandy suggested.

I pinched my lips to the side and shook my head. "No. Let's go ask." I grabbed Mandy's hand and pulled her behind me to Miranda's desk.

"Hey, Miranda, do you have a minute?" I asked.

"Sure," she said. She stopped clicking on her keyboard and looked up at me.

"I hoped you could tell me who delivered the lilies you brought to my classroom. Do you remember the name of the company? Did the delivery-man say who the flowers were from? Did you have to sign anything that would indicate who sent them?" Poor Miranda fell victim to everything I'd learned from being on the receiving end of Mom's multitude of questions.

Mandy elbowed me, and by the time I finished, Miranda's eyes were wide. Mandy jumped in, speaking much more calmly than I had. "Sorry, Miranda. Paige thought she knew who sent the flowers, but she was wrong, so we're trying to figure it out. Any info you have would be helpful."

Miranda looked between us. She bit her lip and tapped her nails across her desk. Then she took a deep breath. "Well, Lorraine left for an early lunch, and I was the only one in the office. Katelyn Ramos had fallen in P.E., and I was cleaning the blood off her knee in the nurse's office when the guy came in." Miranda was sweet, if a bit long-winded. She smiled. "He was really cute," she said. "Light hair, short, spiky in front." Miranda flipped her fingers near the top of her forehead, mimicking the spiky hair.

I grabbed Mandy's arm in a death grip and said one word: "Jake."

Mandy looked at me, then turned back to Miranda. "Did you get a name?"

Miranda shook her head. "Sorry."

"What did he say?" Mandy asked.

Miranda inhaled, and her eyes lit. "He asked if Paige Hall worked here. I confirmed she did, and he asked if I would get the flowers to her."

"That's it?" I asked and squeezed Mandy's arm tighter.

Miranda startled and put a hand to her chest. "Yeah . . . is that okay? I was a little frazzled, you know, with Katelyn's bloody knee and all. Did I say something wrong?"

"No, we were just hoping for a name," Mandy said with a wide smile. She pulled her arm from my grip. "Thanks Miranda."

I stood like a statue while hopeful flutters zipped through my chest. Mandy nudged my elbow and pulled me back to reality. I mumbled my thanks to Miranda, and we turned to walk back to my room.

"I . . ." Miranda began, and we stopped to look back at her. Her hands twisted her long necklace. "I did watch him walk to his car," she said. I realized I was leaning toward her desk. "He got into a gray, sporty sedan." Miranda shrugged. "I don't know if that helps."

I exhaled, and my hope that Jake had sent the flowers blew away with my breath.

"Thanks again, Miranda," Mandy said, and I followed her back to my room as all the happy jitters collided and then careened to the bottom of my stomach.

"It couldn't have been Jake," I said and flopped into a chair. "He drives a black truck."

"And how would he know where you worked?" Mandy asked.

"When we went to dinner, he asked me questions about my job. I might have mentioned which school I worked at," I said.

"But you don't remember?" Mandy asked.

I shook my head and grimaced. "No. Not for sure anyway." I let out a groan. "I was kind of a jerk to Gavin," I told Mandy.

She shrugged it off. "He was definitely a jerk to you. So you're even. Actually, that's a completely false statement. You are still soaring in the clouds over his pathetic cheater self." She examined the flowers one more time. "You're gonna bring these home, right?"

"Fine," I agreed. "I'll see you there."

I lugged the beautiful bouquet to my car and braced it on the floor of the passenger seat between my purse and my gym bag. After depositing everything in the house, I changed and went for a run.

It was my first day testing my ode to simplicity, and already things had become complicated. When I realized Gavin hadn't sent the flowers, I'd wanted the lilies to be from Jake. I didn't expect a relationship, but in a twisted way, I wanted him to feel guilty for ditching on our date.

Everything was in his hands. I refused to call him again because I was done with one-sided relationships. However, if Jake called me and apologized or sent flowers, well then, of course we could talk. His was an apology I would listen to.

I pushed hard the first mile and a half and then slowed as I turned toward home. About one block away from the house a text came in.

Hey,
I hope you like lilies.

My feet slowed, and I stopped to stare at my phone. Jake.

CHAPTER 10
I Grinned

I SKIPPED THE REST OF the way home. Truly skipped. And I grinned the entire time.

A multitude of emotions pounded through my chest: excitement at this possible new beginning, guilt for my snippiness with Gavin, wonder at Jake's thoughtfulness, and remorse for my impatience with Miranda. I needed to work on my tact—empathy was a trait I had yet to master—and I resolved to practice being patient. If I could master this trait, it would help me in my relationships with my mom, my coworkers, and my students—even in my interactions with Jake. If I had known how to be patient, maybe I wouldn't have experienced so much frustration when Jake bailed on our tour-of-the-base date. But thinking about the flowers and his text, I was truly glad to know of his contrition.

When I got home, I sat on the couch and looked the flowers over before texting back, *They're beautiful. I would have thanked you earlier, but there was no card.*

Jake: *Sorry.*

I wondered if he was apologizing for last weekend or for forgetting a card.

Jake: *It seems like I'm always apologizing to you.*

Me: *Um . . . Sorry?*

Jake: *I can't do this . . .*

My elation fizzled, and with my fluctuating emotions, I decided *Simplicity* should be the name of a roller coaster. Then my phone rang, and Jake's number popped up. I took a deep breath and, after two rings, answered.

"Hey." Jake's warm voice floated over the line. "I'm not a huge fan of texting."

Mandy walked by and looked at me sideways. "Who are you talking to?" she mouthed.

I pointed to the flowers. "Jake," I whispered back, and Mandy clapped her hands quietly in front of her.

"Thanks for picking up," he said.

I wasn't sure what to say, so I stayed silent. Mandy walked into the kitchen, giving me privacy.

"So . . . how have you been?" Jake asked.

I'm sure it was an innocent question, a simple conversation starter. But for some reason, it seemed loaded. A sarcastic reply such as "Oh, you mean for the last week or so since you ditched me and haven't called until now?" first popped into my head, but I looked at the flowers and resolved to tap into my reserve of patience. Jake was trying. I could at least be cordial, although I wasn't sure where to take the conversation from there. *Spontaneity, here we go.*

"I'm fine. Did you have a good trip?" I asked.

"*Good* is a relative word. We didn't have any problems, so that part was good, but it was work." Jake paused, then continued. "The part that wasn't good was I kept thinking how much you must hate me."

"My mom always told me *hate* is a really strong word," I said.

Jake laughed lightly. "It is, but I think I may deserve it. I couldn't help getting called in last week—"

"You could have warned me," I cut in.

"Yeah, I should have. I'm usually not such a jerk. I really am sorry," Jake said.

"I know," I said.

"But do you believe me?" Jake asked.

"Have you seen these flowers?" I asked.

"Well, I dropped them off."

"Enough said." I pulled the rubber band out of my hair and leaned back against the couch pillows with a smile. "I believe you."

"Whew," Jake said with a laugh. "Does that mean you forgive me too?"

"Mmm . . ." I stalled, knowing how much I wanted to forgive him and give him a chance. I closed my eyes and debated my answer.

"I'll take you to dinner again. Somewhere nicer than Casa de Taco," Jake said.

"I don't know if food can redeem you this time," I said, and even though I couldn't see Jake's face, I could tell he was disappointed. "Remember in

Greenie's parking lot I suggested you join the PTA?" He softly murmured agreement, and I continued. "How about instead of PTA you come to the career fair?"

"Career fair?" he repeated.

"You can come to my school and tell the kids all about being a pilot and being in the air force. It's next Wednesday after lunch. There'll be all sorts of different occupations, and it's nothing fancy: a few E-Z Ups and tables and some kids walking around, asking questions." I held my breath and waited. I had no idea how Jake felt about kids or community service or if he could get away from work. Sure, he served our country, but maybe he'd signed up for the mere glory of being a pilot. I'd built him up to such perfection in my mind, yet I knew nothing about him beyond basic facts.

Jake was silent.

"Never mind," I said. "December's a crazy time of year, and it's totally last minute. No big deal."

"No, no, Paige, I need to earn my stripes." I heard his phone buzz. "What time should I be there?" he asked.

"Are you serious?"

"Yeah, I just cleared it with my commander."

Mandy walked around the corner and looked at me expectantly. I sat up on the couch. "Things officially start at twelve fifty, but the kids can walk around at lunch too, which starts at twelve."

"Then I'll be there before noon so we can set up," he said. I nodded at Mandy with a goofy grin but froze when Jake spoke again. "I have one condition though. After the fair, I get to take you to dinner."

"Coming to my school can count as your penance. You don't have to take me to dinner."

"Acknowledged. But I'd like to spend some time with you. What do you say?" Jake asked.

Of course I said I'd go to dinner with Jake. My goofy grin was again plastered on my face, and Mandy laughed as she walked back to her food in the kitchen. Jake and I chatted a while longer. I told him about some of the other booths at the fair and promised to introduce him to Mandy. Jake said he'd touch base a day or two before to confirm everything.

After I hung up, Mandy waited an entire ten seconds before emerging from the kitchen with a bowl of pasta in her hand. "So . . . ? What did Mr. Air Force say?"

"Mr. Air Force?"

"Okay, Mr. Romance. Or better yet—Mr. Air Force Romance!"

I laughed. "I don't know why you're asking. You were eavesdropping the entire time." I sat up and threw my pillow at her.

She dodged my weak throw. "True." She smiled and took a bite.

I was too excited to stay mute, so I heated a microwave dinner and rehashed the entire conversation with Mandy. She forced me to acknowledge her brilliance since she had suggested inviting him to the career fair to begin with.

Then she disappeared to grade papers and video chat with Brandon. I showered and put on comfy sweats, then went to the coffee table to admire Jake's flowers once again.

Assuming the lilies were from Gavin had been easy; he'd been so ingrained in my life. However, my rudeness to him was not justified. No matter what new beginning lay ahead, there was no reason my relationship with Gavin couldn't have a happy, or at least a peaceful, ending. I knew it was the end, and after my earlier text, I was pretty sure Gavin knew it too.

I picked up my phone and texted him: *Sorry for being rude earlier.*

Gavin: *Did you find your mystery man?*

I hesitated, hating all the inferences that could be read in a simple text. Did Gavin mean man as in *man* or more as in the general human race? I shook off my reservation and typed *Yes.*

Gavin: *I knew it was a guy.*

I wanted to jump up and ask how, why, what does it matter, but Gavin texted again. *He's lucky, and I meant what I said. I hope you're happy.*

Me: *Thank you.*

In the moment, in that breath, I *was* happy, and I was pretty sure the happiness would last me for the entire week until I saw Jake again. Then I would take it one step at a time. I leaned over to inhale the fragrant lilies and then went to bed with a grin on my face.

CHAPTER 11
I Ogled (along with a Bunch of Other Women)

JAKE SHOWED UP ON WEDNESDAY at precisely 11:45 a.m., decked out in his flight suit and boots, with his blue cap perched on his head. And he looked good. Really good. As Jake filled out the forms for a visitor pass, I noticed the sideways glances Miranda and Lorraine shared. Jake seemed oblivious, but maybe he had grown used to women ogling.

He had brought his own air force–screened E-Z Up, a banner with his squadron name, pamphlets, stickers, patches, pencils, models of two different planes, and another member of his crew, a loadmaster he introduced as Squiggly, although his name tag read Donald Griffith. I would have questioned the guy's nickname, but he didn't contradict Jake, so I figured it was legit.

I asked the janitor to help them unload their gear, and he hooked them up with an electric cart to haul everything out to the blacktop. Jake and Squiggly quickly set up their booth, and when the kids were dismissed for lunch, the men were bombarded. I wasn't surprised the air force pilot was more popular than the dentist, but I did find amusement in the amount of girls talking to Jake. They easily outnumbered the boys.

I watched from afar as Jake and Squiggly answered repetitious questions. They were both patient, explaining the airplane models, using hand signals to demonstrate maneuvers, and passing out the materials they had brought.

Mandy walked up beside me and whistled low. "I know you said he was cute, Paige, but that was a total understatement."

"I won't tell Brandon," I said.

She waved away my comment. "I already told him." She held up her phone. "We just got done talking. And whose idea was this again?" She swept her hand toward Jake and his booth.

"Yours, of course, my brilliant, wise, benevolent friend." I glanced at my watch. "School's out in about ten minutes. Want to meet him?"

Mandy and I walked over to the booth as Jake apologized to a tall skinny boy. "Sorry, man. I'm all out of pencils." Jake looked around, but their stash had been cleaned out. "Tell you what," he said to the boy. He reached his left hand up to his right shoulder, and the Velcro hissed as he pulled one of the patches from his uniform. "Take this."

The boy's eyes lit up. "Really?" he asked.

"Yeah." Jake handed the patch over. "Now you'll have a reminder of which squadron is the best."

The boy murmured his thanks and walked off in a euphoric daze. The final bell rang, and the kids headed out the gates.

Jake put his hands on his hips and looked at me. "I guess we should have planned for more kids," he said.

"You were really generous to give him your patch," I said, and Jake shrugged the compliment away.

Mandy stepped forward. "Adam's a quiet kid, and you just made his day. I think you made a new recruit." She stuck out her hand. "I'm Mandy."

Jake shook her hand and introduced her to Squiggly.

Mandy asked the question I hadn't. "Squiggly?"

"It's my call sign," Squiggly said with a shrug.

"What happened to Maverick or Iceman?" Mandy asked.

I elbowed her, but Jake laughed. "They set the bar high, but the truth is we don't generally pick our own call signs. It's more accurate to say they get assigned," he said.

"So how did you end up with Squiggly? There's gotta be a story there," Mandy teased.

"Yes, ma'am." Squiggly said, and his eyes turned mischievous. "Let's just say when I was a young airman, I didn't realize how difficult it would be to, uh, control my stomach in the back of a plane practicing evasive maneuvers." Mandy and I exchanged a confused look.

"Squiggly got motion sickness a lot when he was training to be a load-master," Jake said. "When he lost his lunch, his instructor admired the handiwork and told him it looked like a bunch of squiggly lines." Jake clapped a hand on Squiggly's shoulder. "The name stuck."

"I really appreciate you coming today, Squiggly, but that's disgusting." I grimaced, then shook the image from my mind.

He laughed.

Mandy turned to Jake and looked at his name tag. "And do you have a call sign, Captain Summers?"

"I do, but perhaps we could save that story for another time," Jake said and reached up to untie the rope holding the banner.

"No way," I said. "You spilled Squiggly's secrets; now it's your turn."

Jake clenched his teeth with a smile and let one side of the banner fall to the ground. He moved to the other rope without answering.

"Squiggly?" I asked. "What's Jake's call sign?"

Squiggly flashed a grin at Jake, then said, "Well, ma'am, Captain Summers outranks me, so I'm not sure I can say. I mean, him being a jackal and all."

Mandy sputtered a laugh and covered her mouth with her hand. "Jackal?"

"As in Jake the Jackal?" I asked. Jake pretended to ignore us, but Squiggly smirked while they collapsed the E-Z Up. "You're not going to tell me how you got your call sign, are you?" I asked, and Jake winked.

The janitor reappeared with the cart, and the men hefted the table and tent onto the back. Squiggly hopped up beside the janitor. "I'll meet you at the truck, sir," he said, then waved and drove away.

"I need to check my lesson plans," Mandy said. "It was nice to meet you, Jake."

Jake shook Mandy's hand again, then turned back to me. "I'll make you a deal. You show me your classroom, and then I'll tell you my story later."

"You do that a lot." I turned and led the way to my room. "Make a deal to get what you want."

We walked inside the building, and Jake swiped the hat off his head and tucked it into his leg pocket. Then he grinned at me sideways. I caught a view of his dimple, and it was adorable. If he knew the power of his smile, he would know he wouldn't need to negotiate any deals. He could broker world peace with a turn of his lips.

I gave him a quick tour of my small room, explaining a few of the kids' favorite activities. I shut down my computer and grabbed a file on a new student, and then we exited through the main office. Jake perched his hat back on his head, and we met Squiggly at a blue truck with military-issued plates.

"You guys went all out today. I appreciate it. The kids loved your booth," I said.

"It was my pleasure, ma'am." Squiggly nodded his head, opened the driver's-side door, and climbed into the truck.

Jake told me he left his car and a change of clothes at his parents'. I thought about offering to drive him there, but our acquaintance was too fresh, so I said nothing. Jake didn't seem bothered. Instead he asked me to follow Squiggly. I jumped into my car, and fifteen minutes later we pulled up to a modest two-level home with a perfectly manicured lawn. Jake's black truck was parked in the driveway.

Squiggly rolled down the window and winked at me as he called to Jake, "I'll see you later, Jackal."

I laughed and waved my thanks as Squiggly pulled away.

Jake shook his head. "Come on."

He knocked twice, then pushed the door open. "Mom? Dad?"

"Come on in," a female voice called.

Jake held the door for me, and I stepped into a small hallway with arched ceilings and a honey-colored hardwood floor. A vase of fresh daisies sat on a small table, and the smell of homemade bread made my stomach turn in hunger. We moved through the hallway to a spacious living room. Natural light flooded through a series of tall narrow windows, and matching honey-colored beams lined the ceiling. A moss-green couch sat in the middle of the room, facing a flat screen mounted on the far wall.

"Hello, sweetie," Jake's mom said as she walked into the room.

Jake's cheeks reddened, but he leaned over and gave his mom a kiss on the cheek. She was average height, with shoulder-length blonde hair. Her narrow face possessed surprisingly round features with soft angles. Her eyes lit when she looked at Jake, but there were dark circles beneath them that she'd tried to mask with concealer.

"Paige, this is my mom." Jake put his arm around the woman and pulled her close.

"Hello, Mrs. Summers. You have a beautiful home," I said. Jake kept his arm around his mom, and my hands hung awkwardly at my side.

"Thank you, dear." She poked Jake in his ribs and stepped out of his reach. "And please, call me Patty."

"Okay," I agreed.

"Come on." Patty grabbed my hand. "You can wait with me while Jake primps." She gave Jake a teasing glance and pulled me toward the kitchen.

I smiled back at Jake, who shook his head and walked down the hallway.

Patty got me a glass of water and insisted I sit while she frosted cinnamon rolls. When she finished, they looked perfect, and I embarrassingly confessed my inadequacies in the kitchen.

Jake didn't take long to change. He walked back in wearing a pair of casual tan pants and a plaid blue-striped button-down. The rich shade of the shirt deepened the blue of his eyes, and when he smiled at me, flutters shimmied in my belly.

"Are you ready?" he asked.

I nodded and slid off the stool. "Thank you, Mrs. Summers—Patty," I corrected myself.

"Enjoy your dinner," Patty said. "And Jake, come back for dessert." She pointed to the cinnamon rolls. "I won't let your father eat all of them. And Lucy will be stopping by. I'm sure she'd love to meet Paige."

"We'll be back in a few hours," Jake told his mother. Then he led me out the front door. "Would you feel comfortable driving together? Or would you prefer to follow me to the restaurant?"

Considering the fact that I'd just met his mother, it seemed silly not to ride together. But I wasn't sure what answer Jake wanted. My gut told me I could trust him, at least to drive me safely to dinner. Then the solution hit.

"How about you ride with me?" I suggested.

"Perfect." Jake followed me to the driver's side and opened my door, then walked around to the other side and climbed in.

He directed me to a small Italian restaurant, and because it was early in the evening, we were seated right away. Once again the conversation flowed easily between us. I commented on how great he was with the kids, and he told me he enjoyed working air shows because he got to share his love of flying with the patrons. He also confessed to enjoying the hero worship that came when he told people he was an air force pilot.

"It's a total ego trip, I know," he said with a shrug. "I'm a pilot. Ego is ingrained in our training."

I was impressed but knew he received more hero worship than most because beyond acting the part, he also looked it. The number of middle schoolers who'd shown a sudden interest in joining the military bordered on comical.

"So you're an egotistical pilot, your mother is a homemaker extraordinaire, your father's a military man . . . and you have a sister?" I asked.

Jake looked at his place setting and smiled. Then he raised his vibrant blue eyes to mine. "My little sister, Lucy, is a florist."

"Ah . . ." I folded my arms across my chest. "Thus, the flowers."

"I still paid for those and picked them out," Jake said defensively. "Lucy said I should send hyacinth and baby's breath." He tilted his head and looked directly into my eyes. "But I thought the lilies suited you better."

A smile twitched on his lips, and I found myself mesmerized, as if frozen in a moment of time. Panic hit. How could he have this effect on me?

I forced my eyes away but couldn't help but ask, "Why? Why did you pick lilies?"

"I'll tell you sometime. But not right now." This time he didn't leave room for me to argue or broker any sort of deal.

The moment snapped, and I blinked myself back to reality. Our food arrived, and I excused myself to wash my hands. When I returned, time resumed. I no longer sat in the shivery air, surrounded by the serene spell Jake cast.

I shook my head clear, and we ate our meal, chatting easily about work and our families. After the waitress cleared our plates, Jake asked if I would mind returning to his house. "My mom's cinnamon rolls are delicious, but I know you have work tomorrow, so if you need to head home, I understand."

I was touched that he gave me an out, but I didn't want to take it. "And pass up homemade cinnamon rolls?" I narrowed my eyes. "I think you just want more for yourself."

Jake laughed. "I'll share. I promise." He paid for dinner, and we drove back to his parents' house.

Jake's dad was every bit as friendly as his wife. Lucy had inherited the same features as her brother—they could practically pass for twins—and she was a delight. She constantly smiled in a sincere way that added to her beauty.

"Here you are, dear," Patty said as she slid a plate with a gooey cinnamon roll in front of me. "If you want more frosting, let me know; I always make extra."

"This is great. Thank you," I said.

Patty served her husband and Lucy, then passed a plate to Jake. "And one for you, too."

"Thanks, Mom." Jake grinned at his mother, then turned to me and winked.

"Of course, sweetie," Patty said. Her nickname for him reminded me of Jake's promise.

"So . . . Jackal?" I asked.

Jake's lips pressed into a tight line, but one side curved up a bit. "I figured I wouldn't get out of it."

"I don't think it could be much worse than Squiggly's story," I said.

"True." Jake chuckled.

"If you won't tell me, I bet Lucy will," I said. Lucy's smile confirmed I was right.

Jake gave a resigned sigh. "Lucy's been sworn to secrecy."

"I bet Paige can keep a secret," Patty said.

"Everyone knew the story behind my call sign back in the day," Mr. Summers said. "Sunshine. Because I was blindingly handsome."

Patty reached over and touched her husband's hand. "And you had such a radiant personality." Mr. Summers beamed.

"From Sunshine to Jackal? This sounds interesting," I said.

"You know everything you hear is classified, right? You can't ever use it as ammo against me for blackmail or any other shady purpose," Jake said.

"Classified, huh?" I laughed. "It's that bad?"

Jake grinned and took a bite.

"Nonsense," Mr. Summers said with a laugh. "Lucy, tell Paige here what happened."

Lucy made a grand show, straightening in her chair and clearing her throat. "Believe it or not, Jake's generally an easygoing guy."

I totally believed it.

Lucy turned to Jake. "Was it your first deployment?"

"Yeah." He leaned forward again and propped his arms on the table. "I was only a second lieutenant." My eyes narrowed slightly, and Jake explained. "I was the new guy, the greenie."

"So his plane has, like, four or five on a crew, depending on the mission, and he started out with one crew and then switched. Am I getting this right so far?" Lucy asked.

Jake nodded. "It was a four-month deployment, and my first crew was awesome. My AC—"

"That means aircraft commander," Patty cut in.

"Thanks," I said.

"Sorry, I forget to speak civilian sometimes." Jake's dimple appeared. "Anyway, my first AC was a veteran pilot, and he taught me a ton. But about two months in, one of the guys had to go home for an emergency, so they switched the crews around."

"So you got a new AC?" I clarified.

"Who was a jerk," Lucy said.

"What happened?" I asked.

Jake inhaled, then blew out his breath. His hands rested on the table, but he didn't speak.

Lucy continued the story. "One of the loadmasters was female. She was a young airman, and she was attractive."

I glanced at Jake and noticed his clenched jaw.

"The rest of the crew started making comments," Lucy said.

"Comments to her or about her?" I asked.

"Both," Jake answered. "They weren't bad at first, but as time went on, they began saying some really degrading things. It's the AC's job to curb that sort of thing, but instead of stopping the comments, he joined in with the other guys." Jake clenched his hands so hard his knuckles turned white.

"Jerk," Lucy said again. Patty reached over and touched Lucy's shoulder. Mr. Summers crossed his arms and leaned back in his chair.

"What happened?" I asked.

"I lost it." Jake looked at me, and his eyes turned solemn. "I got on headset and told them if I heard one more disparaging remark about females, I would turn all of them in for sexual harassment"—he casually lifted one shoulder—"after breaking each of their noses." He attempted a small smile. "They backed off, and I didn't have to address it again. I'm an AC now, and my crews know I don't tolerate that sort of thing, but after that deployment, word got around. So they nicknamed me Jake the Jackal."

My, my, Jake Summers. The many reasons to ogle just kept adding up.

CHAPTER 12
I Tripped, Literally and Figuratively

When Jake walked me out to my car, he asked if I would give him another chance to give me a tour of the base and if I was free on Saturday. He promised he wouldn't get called in or cancel for any reason, so I agreed. He told me I could bring Mandy too, but she was meeting Brandon for the weekend, so it would be only the two of us.

Three days later I found myself driving on the daunting road that led to the military base. Tall flagpoles topped with flags from every state whipped in the breeze. Large brown signs denoted *Threat Level Bravo*, whatever that meant, and a guard stand marked a checkpoint for cars. Jake had told me to meet him at the visitors' center, and I pulled into the lot about ten minutes early.

I was wearing a wide-neck green sweater with jeans and a pair of half boots. The weather had held warm for December, but I'd packed my fleece jacket in my car, just in case. I wasn't sure if I should wait for Jake or head inside the office to do paperwork or fingerprints or whatever was required to get on base. The bench by the door seemed to be the best option, so I headed there to wait.

Before sitting, I decided to take a picture of the Travis Air Force Base sign. Who knew when, or if, I'd ever be back? I liked to freeze momentous occasions in pixelated cyberspace, so I flipped my phone's camera and snapped a selfie.

Then I heard a warm chuckle behind me. "Would you like me to take one for you?"

I spun around to see Jake smiling at me, and my knees got all squishy as my neck flushed red. "No, I got it. Thanks," I said and waved my phone in the air.

"How was the drive?" Jake asked.

"Not bad," I answered and looked him over. He had replaced the flight-suit patch he'd given the boy at school. The memory of his kindness brought a smile to my face. I motioned with my thumb toward the brown building marked *Visitor Check-in.* "So do I need to go sign something?"

"Not if you don't mind leaving your car here. I can drive you around base and bring you back when we're done," Jake said.

"Hmm," I hedged, and Jake raised his eyebrows. "It's just, well . . ." I shifted my purse higher on my shoulder. "After the whole parking-lot thing, I kind of promised myself I wouldn't drive with you."

I was teasing, but after a long silence, I wondered if I'd offended Jake. Thankfully, he surprised me by busting into a hearty laugh. I realized then that I could be myself around Jake, and I liked it.

"Oh man," he said. "You're never going to let me live that down." I gave a halfhearted shrug.

"What about this?" He raised his right arm as if taking an oath. "I promise not to drive over the speed limit and to obey all traffic rules while Paige Hall is a passenger in my vehicle." Then he leaned toward me. He masked his mouth with his hand and whispered in my ear. "The average speed limit on base is twenty-five miles per hour, so I think you'll be safe."

His breath tickled my ear and sent a shiver down my neck.

"Okay," I whispered back, sounding breathless and pathetic. Man, this guy was smooth, and he was sucking me in.

He led me to a car, but it wasn't the truck from the grocery store and Casa de Taco. It was a dark-gray Audi A4 with sporty wheels and snazzy headlights.

"This is yours?" I asked, and Jake smiled at my question. "I mean, it's not what you were driving the other day."

"Yeah, the truck is Lucy's," he said and opened the door for me. "She was blocking me in the driveway that day, so I took her car instead of mine." I mulled that information over while he walked around to the driver's side, pulled off his hat, and climbed in. He started the car and backed out. "Besides," he added, "she begs to drive this. If I use her truck every once in a while, she can claim I owe her and take my car for a spin."

"And you let her?"

He grinned. If I could package his smile to view on demand, I would be a happy woman.

"It's just a car," he said.

Huh. Gavin had never let me drive his car.

Jake pulled up to the base entrance and flashed an ID card at the gun-bearing guard. The man looked a couple of years older than us, but he pulled his shoulders tall, clicked his boots together, and saluted Jake. Jake returned the hand gesture, and we drove through the gate. I smiled and stared out the window, absorbing every detail.

Brown informational placards replaced the green road signs I was accustomed to. The buildings didn't have names or signs explaining their purpose; they were simply denoted by numbers pasted on the outside of their cinder-block frames. Displays of aircraft, a memorial wall, and lots of shrubbery and grass were spread across the vast acreage of the base.

Jake glanced at me a few times. "Should we go to the plane first, or do you want to grab a bite to eat?"

"If you're okay, let's see the plane," I said. I was hungry. My breakfast had been yogurt and one slice of toast. But nerves had filled my stomach and had not left room for much else. They still inhabited a large portion of my insides. I needed food but didn't trust my digestive system to agree with me.

We drove a few more miles until Jake pulled up to another cinder-block cube marked with the numbers 4125. "This is my squadron building," he said. An image of Atlas supporting the world on his shoulders was painted on a large boulder near the door tagged with the words *76th Airlift Squadron*.

Jake parked, and as I began to climb out of the car, he hurried around and held the door for me. "I'm supposed to get that, you know," he said.

"Oh, sorry." I flushed. Of course I knew. Gavin had always opened my door when we walked out to the car. It was one of my requirements for anyone I considered dating, but unlike Jake, Gavin had never opened my door when we arrived somewhere.

Jake smiled. "My mother taught me to be a proper gentleman, so if you don't mind waiting, I'd like to get the door for you."

"I'll practice being patient." I smiled back and then walked with Jake to the door of the building.

"We have to make a quick stop so I can log my time." He punched in a code, then ushered me inside the building before following.

Motivational posters and award plaques hung on plain gray walls. Offices branched out on either side, and everything was extremely quiet.

"Where is everyone?" I asked.

"We usually get weekends off, unless we're on a trip," he explained.

"So I made you come to work when you didn't have to?"

"I offered, remember?" Jake led me to one of the side offices. He pulled out a notebook and scratched a few things inside. "Just one quick call," he said.

He pulled out his phone, and I wandered farther inside the room. There were four cubicles spaced along the walls, and I immediately found Jake's desk. His grin was easily discernible in one of the photos. It was a family picture. He and his parents and younger sister sat on a large boulder with red-rock cliffs rising behind them.

"We're all set," Jake said, stepping up behind me. He nodded toward the picture. "Last year, after I got back from Afghanistan, we took a family trip to Zion."

"Lucy's great," I said, pointing to his sister and glancing up at him.

"Yeah." He tilted his head and smiled at the photograph. "She's pretty cool."

"Like her brother?" I asked.

"I'll leave that up to you to decide." Jake led me out another door, where a guy sat waiting for us in a golf cart. "This is Homer; he's going to take us out to the plane."

"Oh, okay." I climbed into the cart and scooted over to make room for Jake. We cruised down a marked lane on the runway. Huge planes dotted the asphalt, which seemed to stretch for miles. "Do you always take a golf cart to the plane?" I asked.

Homer snorted.

"No. We usually walk." Jake unzipped one of the chest pockets on his flight suit and pulled out a lanyard with a badge and his picture. He looped it over his neck.

I turned to Homer. "Thanks for giving us a ride."

"Anything for Jake the Jackal," Homer said. Jake rolled his eyes.

Huge gray airplanes were parked in lines across the tarmac. The tails were painted with an orange stripe and bore the squadron name. There were numbers and warnings painted in black on the tail, and toward the front of the plane, *United States Air Force* was emblazoned, bold and proud.

Homer turned up one of the aisles and pulled next to the one plane surrounded by movement. The cargo hold on the back of the plane was open and lowered to the ground. Several airmen in camouflage maneuvered about.

"Here we are," Jake said. I stepped off the golf cart and followed his eyes to my brown heeled half boots.

"I guess I didn't wear the best shoes," I said, noticing Jake's sturdy green boots.

"I should have warned you. We'll make it work. Thanks, Homer." Jake hit the top of the golf cart. "Come back in forty minutes, will ya?"

"Sure thing," Homer said and whipped the cart around.

We walked to where the rear of the plane had been lowered. "We'll start in the cargo area, then move up to the cockpit," Jake said and turned toward me. "'Cause that's my favorite part." He grinned.

"Hey, Captain," a younger airman said, then walked away under one of the massive wings.

"Why are there people only at this plane and not at the others?" I asked. "They didn't have to come out just for us, did they?"

"I wish I had that kind of sway," Jake said. "Maintenance is doing some repairs, and my buddy Griz said we could come out."

Jake walked me through the cargo area, pointing out how they load the cargo and explaining the job of the loadmasters. Questions naturally arose because curious gadgets and buttons were everywhere. Jake explained how the plane could transport everything from soldiers to pallets of food to supplies to tanks.

We moved into the cockpit, and Jake pointed out crew positions and had me sit in the left seat. He sat beside me and walked me through the checklist he followed before takeoff.

"Let me know when you've had enough. I could talk planes all day," he warned.

"There are so many buttons and dials. I don't know how you keep it all straight."

"Lots of practice," he said. He pointed to rudder pedals, throttles, and the control stick and showed me which switch lowered the landing gear. "And this is the FMS—Flight Management System. Most everything we need gets displayed on these screens." Jake pointed to a screen positioned directly in front of the copilot's seat, and there was a matching screen in front of where I sat on the pilot's side of the plane.

There were hundreds of buttons. "Aren't you ever tempted to go crazy and push and flip to your heart's content?" I reached over and pretended to press multiple switches.

"I value my life, so I stick to the Dash-1." I looked at him, dumbfounded. He chuckled. "The Dash-1 is our instruction manual," Jake said.

"It's probably as thick as a set of encyclopedias."

"Pretty much." He maneuvered out of his seat and stood on the flight deck. "Come on, let's get Homer to take us back, and we'll grab some lunch."

I extracted my right leg and found secure footing on the narrow aisle between the pilot and copilot seats. Planting my hands near my hips, I pushed out of the seat and pulled my left leg behind me. At least, I tried to. My foot hit what I think was the throttle, and I lurched forward.

A startled scream escaped as I catapulted toward Jake. He stepped back with his left foot to brace his stance, wrapped his arms around me, and pulled me securely into his chest. He craned his neck backward and looked down at me.

"Are you okay?" he asked with an amused smile.

"Other than being completely mortified? Yeah," I said while my cheek pressed against his solid pectoral muscles.

He held me firmly in his arms, and I stood unmoving, shocked at how comfortable I felt in his embrace. I cleared my throat, lifted my head, and raised my hands to his shoulders. I meant to move away, and slowly my fingers trailed the fabric of his flight suit as I leaned back. But Jake's hands remained firm and solid around me.

He searched my face, and the comfort I'd felt before churned with buzzing energy. I didn't know what he wanted. I didn't know what I wanted, so I opened my mouth. "Sorry about that," I said.

And the moment was broken.

Jake released his hold, and I stepped back and straightened my sweater. He asked if my ankle was okay, and after wobbling it back and forth, I told him I was fine. We moved back through the cargo hold, and when we walked down the loading ramp, Jake offered me his hand.

Of course I accepted and was sad when we reached the asphalt and Jake let go. Homer was waiting for us, and on the way back to the squadron building, I asked him how he'd gotten his call sign. He explained that he'd watched way too many episodes of *The Simpsons* and was always throwing out one-liners. When he told me his real name was Bart, I couldn't help but laugh at the irony.

I thanked Homer for the ride, and Jake led me back to the office, where he made another note in the notebook. Then we walked out to his car. "There's a great place to eat on base if you're okay with that."

"Sure," I said.

He pulled his Audi into the parking lot for a building with a fluorescent sign flashing *Bowling Alley*. I looked at him sideways.

"There's a café inside, and they make the best deli sandwiches. I swear." He laughed. "Come on."

He opened my door again, and we headed inside.

I ordered the turkey Christmas special with cranberry sauce, and Jake got an Italian combo with all the fixings. The place was relatively empty, considering it was a Saturday afternoon, and we grabbed a table in the corner.

We took the first few bites in silence. My stomach was grateful to finally be filled with something other than nervous anticipation.

"Thanks for the tour," I said. "I doubt I could recognize the plane in the sky, but now I have a mental image of you in the cockpit. It's amazing something so big can soar through the clouds."

"It's not so hard to pick out. The C-17 is one of the few military planes with wingtips." He wiped his hands on a napkin, then tossed it onto his empty plate. "After the way we met, I didn't expect any hero worship from you," Jake said.

My laugh petered out, but my smile remained fixed.

Jake reached across the table and touched my wrist below the hem of my sleeve. "Your wrist is scratched." His fingers were warm and gentle.

"Oh. I didn't notice." I looked down at my wound.

"I bet it's from when you tripped on the flight deck. You probably scraped it on one of my zippers," he said with a sheepish grin.

I watched his fingers trace the small scrape. His soft and tender touch left me transfixed in the peaceful moment.

It took a lot for me to be comfortable with someone. Gavin had cleared that hurdle. I had dropped my defenses and let Gavin in only to have him break my heart.

Jake had scaled my walls quickly, and the realization startled me once again. I shifted and pulled back. His fingers dropped from my wrist.

The air pressed around us, heavy and thick, a sort of claustrophobic fog. I needed to break out. I forced a smile. "You know this because you've had to catch lots of hapless females while in uniform?"

"No." Jake's lips twitched. "That was a first."

We dumped our trash into the bin, returned to the car, and slowly drove off base. The afternoon had ended too quickly.

"Thank you," I said as Jake turned into the parking spot next to my car.

"I warned you I could talk planes all day."

"It was nice to see what you do." I mindlessly rubbed at the scratch on my wrist.

I stared out the front window, and the moment stretched long and quiet. Jake reached across the console and stilled my fingers.

"Careful. You don't want to infect it," he said.

I looked down at his hand, then up at his eyes. He was looking at me, probably waiting for me to get out of his car. I blinked a few times and reached for the door handle.

"Hey, that's my job, remember?" Jake stepped out and hurried around to open my door.

"Thank you." I got out and fumbled through my purse for my keys as I walked.

"Paige?" he called, and I turned to face him. "I have to go out of town on Tuesday. Can I call you when I get back?"

My hand closed around my keys, and I pulled them from my bag. A smile spread across my face. I couldn't contain my joy even if I tried. "Yeah," I said. "I'd like that." And I was convinced I really would.

The feeling of excitement in my stomach did not dissipate as I got into my car and pulled onto the road. Although our first few dates had been surrounded with apologies, I knew I was falling. I wasn't ready to jump off a cliff or take a momentous step in our relationship, but Jake wasn't asking me to jump. He asked for one day at a time, and no matter how much I tried not to spring forward, being with Jake tripped me up. I was falling, slowly, clumsily, and surely, and I took comfort in knowing that at the end of my fall, Jake stood ready to catch me.

CHAPTER 13
I Confessed

JAKE CALLED THE NEXT EVENING right when I returned from Sunday dinner at my parents'. Heather had quizzed me about my date, and for every question she asked, Mom had asked three more.

"How did the date end?" Heather had asked.

"Did he ask you out again? Did he try to kiss you? Was it dark outside or light when he said goodbye?" Mom had asked. What did the time of the sunset have to do with anything?

I had admitted I hoped to see Jake again. It was a big thing to admit aloud. I enjoyed being with him. I wanted to know more about him, and I wanted the feeling to be mutual. My confession represented a huge step in moving forward.

After telling my mom and sister there had been no kiss, I'd thought about what it would be like to kiss Jake. The thought had stayed with me as we'd moved on to other topics, and after listening to sappy songs on my drive home, a phone call from Jake was the perfect conclusion to my weekend.

"I know I said I wouldn't call until I got back, but I . . . well, I wanted to tell you how much I enjoyed yesterday," Jake said.

"You could have sent a text," I said.

"I'm not much for texting," he reminded me. "I know it's easy and everyone does it, but I prefer a conversation. I think it's more genuine. Texts can bury emotions, and things can be misinterpreted."

Gavin and I had texted frequently. Often, on days when we didn't see each other, we had carried out long conversations via text, and thinking back, sometimes it had felt like we hadn't communicated at all. There was something to Jake's assertion. Conversation served as a better conduit to convey emotion.

"I suppose you're right," I said. "I've never considered it that way before."

"There's definitely a time and place when texting is handy. But I figure if I really want to talk to someone, I should find time to call," Jake said. "I like hearing an actual voice in my conversations, and no, Siri doesn't count." He laughed lightly, then added, "I kind of go off-grid when I'm gone. I wanted to tell you . . . so you wouldn't think I wasn't calling for a different reason."

I'd never considered myself needy, but maybe Jake was right. I probably would have jumped to conclusions about him, about us. I blamed it on the overanalyzing side of the female brain. Jake was telling me he rarely texted and that if he had something to say, he would call. I could deal with that. Did I need a constant string of digital conversation to feel acknowledged? I really hoped the answer was no.

"How long will you be gone?" I asked.

"Eight days."

"And you can't tell me where you're going?"

"Actually, this time I can. We're heading to Japan," he said.

"Wow." Half a world away. It seemed surreal.

"I'm coming down to visit my parents tomorrow before I head out," Jake said. "If you want to join us, my mom's making pie."

"What time?" I asked.

Winter break had officially begun, and I had three weeks off. Mandy had an appointment to get her wedding dress fitted in the morning, and she'd asked me to meet her at her classroom at two thirty to help her sort and label the microscope equipment.

"How about six?" Jake asked.

I couldn't help the excitement that bubbled inside and fizzled up near my lungs. "What kind of pie?" I asked, as if it would help me make up my mind.

"Chocolate pecan," Jake said.

I could help Mandy for a couple of hours. I was certain she wouldn't mind bumping the project to another day to finish. "I'm in," I said.

Jake said he'd meet me at his parents', and the moment we hung up, I began counting down the hours until I saw him again.

Mandy's dress fitting ran late. We only got through half a box of microscope parts before I had to leave to meet Jake. She had a lot more work than I realized. I left her sitting at a lab table with three more boxes to sort and a promise to help her finish the next day.

Jake's invitation had been for pie, but with the holiday around the corner, I wanted to arrive with something in hand. Since I didn't drink, alcohol was out of the question, and flowers would seem lame since Lucy would be there. I decided to bring a basket of homegrown lemons and grapefruits from my parents' yard and braced myself for Mom's interrogation.

Thankfully, she asked minimal questions, and they centered on why I'd chosen to bring citrus rather than flowers. After explaining that Lucy owned a floral shop, Mom got excited and asked me to let her know where it was located.

I ate a quick dinner with my parents and then freshened up before heading over to the Summerses' house.

Jake answered the door with a grim expression. "Paige?" he said as if he were surprised to see me. He stepped outside and closed the door behind him. "You must not have gotten my text."

My stomach turned, and the basket of fruit suddenly seemed heavy. "You said you didn't text. I didn't think to check my phone," I said, my voice a bit tart.

Jake looked back at the door, then down at my simple offering. He sighed and asked, "Can we go for a walk?"

I clenched my teeth and pressed my eyes closed. I opened them again and said, "No, Jake, it's okay. It's obviously a bad time. I'll go."

He reached forward and touched my arm. "I don't want you to go. But I do need to explain. Here." He took the basket from my hands and stepped back toward the house. "Wait here a second while I grab a sweatshirt."

I'd left my jacket at home because I figured we'd be inside. I rubbed my hands up and down my arms, and Jake stepped back outside a moment later holding two sweatshirts.

"I thought you might need one too," he said, and he held the fleece hoodie while I stuck my arms into the sleeves.

"Thanks." I pulled up the zipper.

"It's Lucy's." Jake shrugged into his sweatshirt and held out his hand.

I looked at his open invitation, torn. Uncertain. Scared. I'd recently wandered from battle, and Gavin had left wounds. My heart was guarded, turning in on itself because my still-fresh experience had taught me that trusting hurt. Taking Jake's hand would turn my heart outward again, and between canceled plans and feelings of uncertainty, the signs warned me to walk away, to remain closed off.

Yet, the only sign that mattered was the one coming from Jake. He watched me with understanding. He extended his hand as an offering, but there was no pressure to take it. The decision was mine to make, and something inside me couldn't resist. I slowly put my hand in his, and his fingers gently folded over mine.

Jake's lips slowly lifted into a smile, and the dimple in his cheek appeared. He led me to the sidewalk, and we walked the length of the block in silence.

Finally, Jake spoke. "My mom's sick." He glanced over at me and continued. "She was diagnosed with ovarian cancer about four years ago, and after surgery the doctors said the tumor hadn't metastasized, but they prescribed some tough chemo. They thought they got everything and hoped my mom would go into remission, but the cancer came back."

I reached my free hand across my stomach and touched his arm.

Jake gave a sad smile, then turned forward again. "About six months ago they realized the tumors had spread throughout her abdomen. She's back on chemo, but . . ." He cleared his throat and pressed his lips tight.

"I'm sorry, Jake," I said and stopped walking. "I really am. Your mother seems like a kind woman."

Jake stared into the darkness. "She always tries to be happy and out-going. But when she's in pain, she can't fake it, and she doesn't want people to see her when she's not at her best."

"I understand," I said and squeezed his hand. "Thank you for sharing something so personal with me."

Jake turned to look at me. His normally vibrant blue eyes were darkened by shadows from the scattered streetlights, but he still held my gaze, and I couldn't look away.

The tension in his face softened. He captured my free fingers and swung both of our hands between us. "This is the second time something I've planned has gone horribly wrong."

"This is out of your control," I said.

Jake blew out a breath. "My mom . . . she's suffered enough. I don't understand why she has to go through this again."

All sorts of explanations came to mind. *We have to trust God's timing. The hard times help us better appreciate the good. God has a reason.* But none of those things felt right. In the end I said, "I'll pray for her."

"Maybe your prayers will work better than mine," Jake said. I opened my mouth to dispute his statement. But Jake squeezed my fingers and said, "I really like you, Paige, and I don't want my crazy life to scare you away." His sincerity touched me, and I suddenly wanted to reciprocate.

"Can I make a confession?" I asked, pulling our hands higher between us.

Jake narrowed his eyes and asked, "Is this a confession I'm going to regret hearing?"

My chest tightened, and I blew out the breath I'd been holding. "I hope not. But if we're putting all of our cards on the table, I think it's something you should know."

"Okay, out with it." Jake flipped my hands around and held them against his chest.

I swallowed. "I was in a pretty serious relationship until about six weeks ago." I looked down at my shoes. "I caught Gavin cheating, and . . ." I let out a strangled laugh. "It really hurt." Jake's thumbs pressed across the backs of my fingers, and I looked back up at him. "You caught me off guard at the grocery store, and to be honest, it's been hard for me to do this. To be here." I shook my head. "I'm glad you told me about your mom, and I'm honored you felt you could trust me. I can handle the trips and the no-texting thing, but I need you to be up-front. Lay it all out for me like you did tonight so I don't keep getting blindsided."

"Phew!" Jake said, tilting his head toward the sky and then back down again. His grin grew. "I thought you were going to tell me you hated to fly or you were half alien or something."

"Jake!" I freed one of my hands and swatted his arm.

He smiled wide. "For the sake of honesty, can I just say that this Gavin guy must be an idiot to let you go?"

I shrugged and looked at our hands that were still clasped while a small smile spread across my face. "He wanted to try to work things out, but I refuse to let him hurt me again. It's over between us." I looked back up at Jake.

"Which is good news for me," he said.

He pulled me closer and raised his free hand to the side of my face. All of the doubt I'd harbored about moving forward with Jake evaporated as he leaned forward and pulled me to him. Our bodies pressed together, and he leaned his cheek against my forehead. His breath stirred my hair, and the moment was filled with subtle perfection.

Jake kept hold of my hand as he walked me back to his house. "I can ask my mom if she's up for visitors now," he offered.

"No, no," I said. "Tonight's been good. I'm content."

"Me too." He squeezed my hand one more time, and as I climbed into my car, he called, "Good night, Paige. Sweet dreams."

CHAPTER 14

I Tipped

WE MET FOR DINNER A few days before Christmas. Jake gave me a beautiful floral stationery set from his trip to Japan, and I gave him a box of specialty peanut brittle and a collection of jackal Christmas ornaments I'd found online. We spent Christmas with our individual families. Over New Year's, Jake had another work trip, but his gifting became a habit. Every time he went on a trip, he brought something back for me. He claimed it was his way of apologizing for being gone, although I quickly saw how much he enjoyed his work. He told me he loved his missions but road trips were hard. He used to enjoy living out of a suitcase, visiting different parts of the world, and flying for hours on end. He still loved the flying, but he preferred his mom's cooking to eating on the road, and since Patty's cancer had returned, he detested being gone.

Whenever Jake's mom was up for company, we spent time at his parents' house. Jake's work schedule kept him busy, so we went on only a few dates, but I was okay because he always made our time together special. He took me horseback riding and hiking. He signed us up for a cooking class at a restaurant and brought some of his mom's homemade brownies in case ours didn't turn out. We ended up eating dessert twice that evening. Jake's culinary skills easily exceeded mine.

A few weeks later, Jake got called in on alert, but then the mission was canceled, so he got the rest of the day off and wanted to spend it with me. It was Heather and Greg's anniversary, and Heather had asked me to babysit. I hadn't seen Jake in a week, so I asked my sister if Mom could cover instead. Heather didn't love Mom's babysitting, because she never put the kids to bed on time and they were always grumpy the next day.

"Please!" I begged my sister. "I'll call Mom and tell her she has to strictly follow your schedule."

Heather begrudgingly agreed, and I set it up with Mom. When I told Jake I was free, he told me he'd pick me up after work and to dress for the outdoors.

He pulled up in Lucy's truck. "I think you're gonna like this," he said.

"What are you up to?" I grinned and let him take my hand and lead me to the truck.

He shook his head as he held my door. "You don't get to know just yet," he said before closing my door, walking around, and climbing in. "But you do get to pick your favorite fast food for dinner."

I folded my arms across my chest and offered a faux pout. "Fine. Hamburgers."

"Hamburgers it is." Jake drove to a nearby fast-food joint and ordered two cheeseburgers with fries. Then he continued to a nearby campground. He unloaded firewood, a double-seater camp chair, and a cooler from the back of the truck. The air turned brisk as we ate our dinner, but afterward Jake built up a fire.

He walked to the truck and returned with a large thick blanket. "This should keep us warm."

"I think you just want to snuggle," I said.

"Busted." Jake shrugged. "Unless you want this all to yourself." He held up the blanket with a teasing glint in his eye.

"Nope. I'll take you and the blanket." I stood, and Jake secured the blanket around both of us before we sat back down. He wrapped his arm around my shoulders, pulling me into his side. His very warm, solid, comfortable side.

"Let me know when you want dessert," Jake said. "I brought stuff so we can make s'mores."

"I thought this was dessert." I shimmied myself closer to him, and he chuckled like I thought he would. "I'm perfectly content. No s'mores needed," I assured him.

"*Perfectly* content?" Jake looked at me, the shadows from the fire tickling his face, and his expression turned solemn.

I considered the weight of his question, but truth was truth. "Yes. Perfectly content." His lips twitched, and his dimple appeared with his smile. The view made my heart happy. "What about you?" I asked.

The dancing firelight made Jake's normally blue eyes appear gray and mystical. He leaned near, his face only inches from mine. "Can I show you how content I am?"

His warm breath washed across my cheeks, and where I'd felt cold only moments before, I now felt heat pulsing through my veins. In response to his question, I tilted my chin upward and closed my eyes.

Jake's lips were soft, gentle, pressing against my own as he kissed me slowly again and again. My heart sped, and I leaned my body in to his. Jake's free hand cradled my cheek, and I raised my hands to his chest, where I grabbed his coat and pulled him even closer. The heat from our kisses warded away the cold. The sincerity in Jake's lips vanquished my fears. He treasured me. And I liked him. A lot. And everything in that moment felt right. The tenderness of his mouth against mine, the care he took with each and every kiss, and the way he pressed me to him paralleled my growing feelings. Kissing him quenched a thirst, a longing. It fulfilled a need I didn't know existed.

He broke away with a final lingering kiss. His breaths came rapidly, and his hand stroked my face. He held my gaze; he claimed my heart. "Perfectly content," he said.

My desire to keep things simple kept me grounded, although sometimes it was hard. I missed Jake when he was gone. It helped knowing he was thinking about me. The gifts he brought were always thoughtful. Overall, I was happy. Jake seemed happy. Only my mom found reasons to complain.

"I never see you anymore," she said.

"Mom, I'm standing in your kitchen," I said and held up the dish I was washing at the sink.

"That's not what I mean," Mom said, and she actually rolled her eyes. "You used to come by at random times, just to say hello or to visit. You never stop by nowadays."

"I've been busy." I loaded the last dish and filled the soap dispenser in the dishwasher. I clicked the door closed and started the cycle, then turned to look at my mom.

"You make time to stop by the Summerses'," she said.

Ah, that's what this was about. "Jake wants to spend time with his mom. You can't fault him for that," I said defensively.

"I wasn't faulting Jake," Mom said, and her look held a challenge. "In fact, I've only met him once. It's hard to judge someone when you hardly know them."

Mom had met Jake when he had asked me to lunch last minute once. Mom and I had been out shopping, so she had driven me to meet him, and I'd introduced the two of them while we waited for a table. Jake had asked Mom to join us, but she'd had groceries in the car and had excused herself to head home. I wasn't sure what more she wanted.

I dried my hands on a dish towel and folded it back up. "Don't go there, Mom. I see you at church, and I take time to come to your family dinners every Sunday." I set the towel on the counter and walked past her.

She followed me into the living room. "Thank you for taking time to grace *our* family dinner with your presence, Paige. I guess I'm old-fashioned to expect anything more." Mom turned to my sister. "And, Heather, you're probably expecting too much to think Paige has time to come babysit."

"I can't do this," I murmured to myself. "Good night, Heather, Greg, kids. Bye, Matt. Bye, Dad." I leaned over and kissed my dad's cheek.

He looked between my mom and me.

"Taking off already?" Matt asked.

But before I could answer, Mom did. "Don't worry, Matt. She'll pencil us in every Sunday, unless Jake calls first. Oh, and if there's an emergency, she might call then too."

In my ode to simplicity, I kept my mouth shut and let the slamming door speak for me. But when I got home, I vented it all to poor Mandy.

"Why does my mom act like that?" I turned and paced in front of the TV. "I'm twenty-five; is there a reason I need to call her every single day?"

"Maybe because you used to? I think she likes when you call her for things." Mandy said from her seat on the couch. After a quiet minute she asked, "Remember how you told me things with Gavin became routine?"

I nodded. "Yeah. But I broke the routine when I broke up with him."

"I don't know that you did, Paige," Mandy said and closed the book she'd been reading. "I know you don't get to see Jake a lot, but the moment he calls, you put everything else on hold. Your friends and family suddenly take second place."

"That's not true." I glared at her.

Mandy leaned back, crossed her arms, and tilted her head. "Really?"

"Yeah, you said it yourself—he's gone a lot. We have to take advantage of the time he's around," I said.

"I understand. But that doesn't mean you can expect everyone else to shift and bend their schedules to accommodate you," Mandy said. My eyes narrowed farther, and Mandy threw up her hands to halt my rebuttal. "I'm just saying that you've bailed on Heather, you've bailed on me, and I'm sure your mom feels you've bailed on her." Mandy held her ground, but I saw the hurt in her eyes.

"What are you saying?" I asked softly.

Mandy sighed, then motioned to the empty cushion beside her. I walked over and sat down. "I like Jake. I like Jake for you. But I think you would do anything for him, and it scares me because I don't know if he'd do the same for you." She paused for a beat. "So prove me wrong. Next time Jake calls, tell him you can't accommodate him. See if he'll change his plans for you."

"Why?" I asked.

"Because you need to know if he'll be flexible for you the way you are for him. You're falling hard, Paige, and I don't want to see you get hurt." Mandy put one hand on my arm. "One of the things that makes you great is that you go all in. You give everything. But I don't think you realize how dangerous that is. In the best relationships, both people give—otherwise one person becomes drained, and the scales tip. When one person gets off-balance, it doesn't work."

"Do you think that's what happened with Gavin?" I asked quietly. "Did he cheat because we weren't balanced?"

"I don't know why he cheated," Mandy said. "But I do know the scales were tipped because he never gave back. I don't want that to happen again."

I knew Mandy was trying to look out for me, but she didn't know Jake. She didn't know how good he was and how well he treated me. So what if I tipped the scales and weighed them down on my side? Giving seemed the natural thing to do for someone you liked. Perhaps Gavin hadn't appreciated it, but Jake did. Didn't he?

I raised my chin and looked her squarely in the eyes. "Fine. Jake gets back on Friday. When he calls, I'll tell him I'm not available. But you'll see; he'll be willing to bend. He'll prove you wrong."

Mandy frowned at my defensiveness. "I hope he does, Paige. I really do," she said.

For the next five days I stewed over Mom's accusations and Mandy's challenge. There were moments I was certain Jake would drop everything for me, but then I would remember the times he hadn't. I didn't really expect him to stiff Uncle Sam. His job was important and didn't leave him room to fidget. He wasn't picking something over me; he was just doing what had to be done. So if he had an option, he would choose me . . . right? He had come to the career fair and always brought me thoughtful gifts. But I hadn't asked him to give up something or change plans for me. Making the request would be new territory for both of us, and the concern in Mandy's eyes when she'd issued her challenge haunted me.

Late Friday night I got a text from Jake. *Just got home and still have to debrief. Will it be too late to call later?*

Me: *No. Glad you're home safe.*

Mandy's stipulation applied to going out. I deemed staying up late on a Friday night to talk to Jake perfectly acceptable. Mandy hadn't broached the topic again, but I'd thought long and hard about what she'd said. In theory, the whole scale analogy made sense. Relationships needed balance. Obviously, Mandy had found her zen with Brandon, and Heather was balanced with Greg. Was that how they'd known they should get married?

I knew Heather had stayed up late helping Greg type papers when he'd worked on his thesis, and she'd still gotten up early every morning to make him a homemade breakfast before he left for work. On the flip side, Greg was always willing to watch the kids and give Heather a night out with the girls. I'd seen Mandy slave in the kitchen for two hours making Brandon's favorite snickerdoodle cookies, and Brandon had tutored Mandy's brother when he'd fallen behind in his calculus class.

Maybe it all came down to balance, each side giving to keep the scales even. I'd always wanted an organic relationship, where neither person had to be something more but instead where being together meant I was something better. Jake and I weren't to the point where he improved me or I him, but he made me smile.

If Mandy was right and I was doing all the giving, my relationship with Jake wouldn't last, and the one thing I knew was I didn't want it to end. It was time to find out if Jake could flex and bend for me the way I did for him.

His name popped up on my phone at ten thirty.

"Hey," I answered.

"Sorry it's so late," Jake said. "I thought you might be asleep and I should wait until morning, but I was looking forward to talking to you tonight."

"I'm glad you called." I saw no harm in admitting the truth. "How was your trip?"

"Long. Did you have a good week?"

"Overall, yeah. Except I missed you." My heartbeat quickened when I said the words. It was the most intimate confession I'd made, and I realized I'd just weighed the scales heavily down on my side.

Jake didn't hesitate before responding. "I missed you too."

The scales immediately balanced, and I smiled knowing that for now, we were even.

Jake shared bits and pieces of his trip. It had become habit for him to give me clues about the souvenir he'd brought me, but he kept his clues so vague I had yet to guess right. We talked for almost an hour before I yawned audibly, and Jake apologized again for keeping me up. Then he asked if he could take me to the orchestra on Saturday. The moment of truth had arrived, the one where Jake could prove my mom and Mandy wrong.

"I'm not able to go Saturday," I said. Then, without thinking, I asked, "Could you come to my family dinner on Sunday instead?"

I pinched my eyes closed. Out of all the alternatives I could have proposed, why did I choose my family dinner?

Jake grew silent, and as the quiet stretched on, my confidence crumbled.

"Jake?" I asked.

"Yeah, sorry. I was thinking through my calendar. What time on Sunday?"

"Five thirty." My voice shook, but I doubted he noticed.

I heard him exhale, and then he answered. "I'm not sure I can make it, Paige. Can I talk to my dad and let you know tomorrow?"

"Sure," I said flatly.

"Maybe . . ." Jake began, and then he stopped. "Never mind. I'll call you tomorrow, okay? Good night."

I mumbled a response, then hung up quickly. Had I really read Jake so wrong? I'd thought he was different from Gavin. Maybe Jake's crazy work schedule and his stunning eyes had turned me around enough that I'd ignored the signs. No matter how much I told myself not to care, an ache in my chest grew. I'd thought we had a chance, but the scales had tipped, and the one person who could balance them out didn't seem to care enough to try.

CHAPTER 15
I Apologized (Twice)

I DIDN'T CONFESS TO MANDY. She would know soon enough. I ate a quiet breakfast and afterward headed to the gym. On the bulletin board near the door, I saw a flyer advertising the orchestra performance Jake had invited me to. The tickets were expensive, and I wondered if he'd already purchased them. The stinging burned anew. I wanted to go with him. I wanted to be with him, but I had tested Mandy's theory, and Jake hadn't flexed. I pushed myself at the gym and worked out hard, forcing my frustration out through the pain in my muscles.

When I got home, I went straight to cleaning the house: deep, intense, scrubbing-the-grout-with-a-toothbrush cleaning. Mandy asked if she could help, but I knew she was scheduled to meet with the wedding director at the site she and Brandon had chosen for the ceremony, Dunlap Gardens. I shooed her out the door and began wiping down baseboards.

Two hours later there was nothing left to clean. I collapsed onto the couch and let exhaustion sweep my mind into sleep. I woke to a tingling in my back and realized I'd fallen asleep on my phone. When it vibrated again, I picked it up and saw Jake's name.

He'd called, precisely as he said he would. He hadn't let me down in that regard. He followed through with whatever he committed to. I wondered if he was committed to me. There was only one way to know, so I answered the phone.

"Hello," Jake said. "How's your morning been?" His voice sounded tentative. I guessed, after our conversation last night, he'd figured out I wasn't too happy. In a way, I was glad to hear his uncertainty.

"I've been cleaning," I answered simply.

He cleared his throat. "Well, Dad said my mom's doing okay, so if your offer still stands, I'd love to join your family for dinner tomorrow."

I rubbed the sleep from my eyes and sat up to make sure I understood. "You want to come tomorrow?"

"Yeah. I mean, if you want me to."

"Of course I do," I said.

I felt like such a fool. I'd spent the last twelve hours blaming Jake, accusing him of not giving, not trying, not caring. It seemed spontaneity was best applied to food choices or movies, and when it came to Jake, I needed to practice patience. After twelve hours of a churning stomach, I now had a clean house, very sore muscles, and a date to bring to family dinner.

Mom and I hadn't spoken since our argument the previous week, and I wasn't ready to admit fault. Mom's accusations had been directed at me, whereas Mandy's had targeted Jake. Mom had meant to hurt me in order to guilt me into the behavior she wanted from me. Mandy's accusations had hurt too, but she'd shared them because she was looking out for me. Obviously, my relationship with Mandy was much more balanced than my relationship with my mother.

I chickened out, and instead of calling, I texted Mom and Dad that I had invited Jake to dinner. As an afterthought, I asked if it would be okay. When Dad responded that Jake was welcome and asked me to bring drinks, I knew Mom still harbored a grudge, or she would've been the one to text.

I shot off a quick text to Heather, begging her to help run interference if necessary. She didn't answer right away, which was unusual for my sister. She didn't text back until after dinner, when Mandy and I sat at our table, addressing wedding invitations. Her text read, *We finally get to meet your mystery man?*

Me: *Yeah—I know I'm crazy to bring him to dinner, but I hoped you and Greg could help me out.*

Heather: *I can't make any promises. The kids have been crazy lately.*

Me: *We'll stick Matt on kid duty and double-team Mom.*

Heather: *She's not as bad as you make her out to be. She just has a hard time not being a mom. Maybe you should give her a chance and not be so hard on her.*

I stared at my phone.

"What's up?" Mandy asked.

"I thought Heather would have my back tomorrow, but she's totally defending my mom," I said.

Mandy checked another name off her invite list. "I know Jake came through for you, and I'm glad. Maybe him coming to your family dinner is the key to fixing your relationship with your mom."

"The whole balance thing?" I asked sarcastically.

"Exactly," Mandy said. Then she pinned me with a stare before adding a sealed envelope to the top of our growing pile.

My phone chimed again.

Heather: *You're mad at me now, huh?*

Me: *No. Just pondering—see you tomorrow.*

Heather signed off with a kissing, smiling emoji.

I looked at the clock and realized I could be listening to classical music with Jake holding my hand. My shoulders sagged, and I began addressing the next invitation.

Jake showed up at five fifteen. We loaded the juice I'd bought into his car, and I directed him to my parents' house. Matt answered the door and took the bag from Jake while I introduced him to my family.

Jake received handshakes, smiles, and pleasantries all the way around. He got a warm reception. Me—not so much. Mom gave me a stiff hug, Heather followed her fake smile with a look of challenge, and Greg seemed confused about how to keep the scales balanced in favor of his wife. He watched our interaction and settled for a wave from across the room. Only Matt and Dad offered genuine hugs, and a tiny morsel of guilt began twining through my ribs.

As soon as Dad had sliced the roast and everyone was served, Jake was flooded with questions. The men asked about Jake's plane and the combat missions he'd flown. He shared a few stories I hadn't heard before, but I recognized how he deflected a lot of questions. I knew from talking with him there was a lot he couldn't share, but instead of shutting down Matt or my dad, Jake would give general answers or tell a story he'd heard from someone else or seen in the news.

Heather and my mom asked more domestic questions about where Jake lived, how military benefits worked, and whether he served with a lot of females. Jake answered everything like a pro, and right when I worried he might be getting overwhelmed, he turned to me and flashed a smile that lit his eyes. I knew then that Jake would be okay, and I enjoyed the rest of my meal.

Jake insisted on helping with dishes, which meant Matt and Greg had to step up too. Heather and I directed the men in the kitchen while Mom and Dad entertained the little ones.

Afterward Jake and I played two rounds of Go Fish with Amelia. Mom set homemade chocolate-chip cookies on the table, and Jake immediately snatched one up.

He took a bite and murmured his approval. "Mrs. Hall, these cookies are amazing. They taste every bit as good as my mother's, and that's not a compliment I give lightly."

Mom smiled and colored a bit. "Thank you, Jake. How's your mom?"

I'd told my family about Patty's cancer, but I doubted Jake wanted to discuss it over dessert. I looked at Mom, hoping to let her know I was grateful she'd asked such an open-ended question, and when we made eye contact, she gave me a knowing smirk. Obviously, she knew my concerns and had worded her question so Jake could fill in the details he wanted to share. Her lips pressed upward into a smile as she listened to Jake's response.

"She's doing great; thank you. She turned fifty-nine today." Jake glanced at me and grimaced. "Oh, I probably shouldn't have shared her age," he said. "Don't rat me out, Paige."

I stood from the table and clutched my hands to my chest. It felt as if a giant vacuum had sucked the air from my lungs.

"It's her birthday today?" Heather asked. "Are you not celebrating as a family?"

Jake polished off his cookie and pushed to his feet. "We went out yesterday and sang to her at the restaurant, then headed to the orchestra. They always perform their winter concert around her birthday, and she loves going. It's become a sort of tradition." He shrugged and continued. "My dad will probably make her a cake tonight, but I gave her my gift yesterday."

Tears pricked the backs of my eyes. The room grew quiet.

Jake looked at me, his head cricked sideways. "You okay?" he asked.

"I didn't know," I whispered. My breathing became cumbersome and heavy, and I blinked rapidly to keep the tears from falling.

Jake glanced around the room and opened his mouth to say something, but nothing came out.

"Amelia, come help me pick up these toys," Heather said. "Matt, can you help Greg get the kids ready to go?"

Mom jumped right in and turned to Dad. "Nathan, come help me dish up some leftovers for the kids to take home."

My family really was great. The room cleared out, and a tear slipped from my eye. I collapsed into the closest chair, and Jake came to kneel beside me. Lifting my hand from my lap, he asked, "What's wrong?"

"Why didn't you tell me it's your mom's birthday?" My voice rattled with emotion.

"You said you couldn't come to the concert, and I didn't want to make you feel bad," he said.

"Oh, Jake," I said. I lifted my hand to the side of his face. "I'm so sorry."

"I just told you I don't want you to be sorry. I don't want you to be sad." Jake brushed another tear from my cheek, and then he took both of my hands and pulled me to my feet. He wrapped his arms around me and held me close. "Don't cry, Paige."

I stood there, so comfortable in his embrace, yet knowing I needed to break away and confess to him once again. "Jake." My voice cracked. I inhaled and started again. "I should have gone with you last night. I told you I couldn't for purely selfish reasons."

"What do you mean?" he asked, and his eyes churned deep blue.

He rubbed his thumbs over the backs of my hands, and I let the soothing motion draw the truth out of me. I told Jake about my fight with my mom and about Mandy's accusations. I explained the entire scale analogy and how I needed to know if we were balanced.

I stared at the buttons on Jake's shirt and offered my weak explanation. "I didn't believe it was true. I knew you were different from Gavin, but Mandy had all these examples, and for some stupid reason, I felt the need to test her theory. I'm so sorry. I took you away from your mom when she's sick, and I passed up a chance to wish her happy birthday." I watched Jake's chest rise and fall, afraid of the anger I would see when I lifted my eyes to his.

After a minute he whispered my name. "Paige?"

I bit my lip and looked at him.

"Did I pass?" he asked.

"What?"

His mouth twisted into a grin. "Did I pass your test?"

My heart melted. "With flying colors," I said.

Jake closed the distance between us, first kissing my temple, then leaning down to kiss my lips.

Matt coughed loudly behind me, and I smiled as Jake released his grip. Mom and Dad walked out of the kitchen and looked at us expectantly.

"If you don't mind, Mr. and Mrs. Hall, we're going to go wish my mom a happy birthday," Jake said.

"Of course," Mom answered. "And I made a plate of cookies to send with you. Please give her our best."

We said a quick round of goodbyes, and within minutes we were driving to the Summerses' house. Jake reached for my hand and squeezed gently.

"Thanks for sharing your family with me," he said.

"I should have done it a long time ago," I said, and for the first time, it hit me that Mom had been right. I determined to call her first thing in the morning and apologize to her as well.

CHAPTER 16
I Fell

JAKE AND I SPENT A pleasant evening with his family. Patty's exhaustion from the night before carried over to our visit, so we stayed for about an hour, sang Happy Birthday one final time, and then said good night.

Jake stared at the road as he drove me home, and I could tell he was contemplating something. I also knew the man sitting beside me was stuffed with goodness. After my major blunder, Jake could have been angry or bitter; he had every right to turn away. Instead he'd wanted to know if he had passed my test. My stupid, pathetic, selfish test. I didn't want to be selfish anymore. Another look at Jake confirmed I was falling fast. His easy demeanor, his patience, and his kind heart all made the fall exhilarating. His physique didn't hurt either.

I trailed my fingers across his bicep to get his attention. "Care to share?" I asked.

The tension in his face faded when he glanced at me. "Just thinking about my mom."

"You could have told me it was her birthday," I said. The guilt for my foolish test washed over me again. When I got home, Mandy was going to split this self-incrimination right down the center and share the guilt with me. "I would have understood. It's important to take every opportunity you have with her."

Jake laughed lightly. "She says the same thing about you." He looked at me again, and I narrowed my eyes in question. "My mom knows I like you. She also knows military life is unpredictable. Whenever I offer to come over and help with anything, she shoos me away and tells me to take time to be with you."

"She's a good woman," I said.

"Yes, she is." Jake pulled into my driveway and told me to stay put while he walked around and opened my door. He extended his hand and lifted me from my seat. He twined his fingers with mine, and we walked toward my house.

"So you like me, huh?" I asked as we stepped up to the front door.

"A lot," he said. I laughed as Jake twirled me under his arm and pulled me close.

I didn't want to break the moment. I stared at him and grinned stupidly. His smile straightened, and he spoke again. "I'm not mad about yesterday, and I understand your need to know where I stand, but can we agree that honesty goes two ways? I promise I will be honest with you, but you have to reciprocate. If you want to know something, you can't be afraid to ask me. Okay?" He leaned forward and kissed my temple. "Mandy's right; we have to find balance, and if our relationship is going to go anywhere, we have to be able to trust one another."

"I know." I leaned in to Jake, nestling my head beside his chin. "I'm sorry," I whispered.

We said our goodbyes, and after Jake walked to his car, I closed the door with a contented sigh. My heart felt lighter than it had in a long time. Jake and I were in a good place. I got ready for bed and fell asleep thinking of where that path might lead.

Jake's trip the following week got canceled. Rather than flying, he worked his desk job at the base—something to do with regulations and currencies and a bunch of military acronyms and other phrases I didn't understand. He split his free time between his mom and me, and while I felt guilty for his extended commute, I cherished our time together.

Because we both worked long days, we kept our dates simple. We ordered takeout or cruised the bookstore, and I made him watch the short version of *Pride and Prejudice* because I figured the ego of a pilot mirrored Mr. Darcy's. I wanted to watch Jake's reaction when Darcy finally confessed his feelings for Miss Elizabeth Bennet, but when that particular scene played, Jake seemed more interested in tangling his fingers in my hair and kissing random places on my face than watching the movie. I was too content to complain. He did laugh at Heather's and my favorite line comparing men to rocks and mountains, and he watched the movie without grumbling. Neither Mandy nor Heather could claim the same support from their significant others—more points for Jake, although he didn't need them.

One night he suggested we go to dinner with my parents. Since Jake's appearance at our family dinner, something in Mom had mellowed. Maybe she'd pulled back because of Patty's illness. Maybe she'd realized I could take responsibility for my own life. There were multiple maybes; however, after the Sunday dinner fiasco, I had called Mom to apologize and to thank her for giving Jake and me space to talk and making a plate of cookies for Patty. After that phone call, our relationship had changed. The scales still hung precariously uneven, but I felt we would now tip for one another. We would support one another and adjust to each scenario we were given.

Because of my truce with Mom, dinner with my parents turned out to be pleasant. Enjoyable even. Any questions Mom asked were . . . normal. Watching Jake toss around stories with my dad and eagerly work to please my mom proved surprisingly relaxing.

The next week Jake flew out on Monday. When he landed in California on Thursday, he got a call from his dad. Patty's pain had become unbearable, and she'd been admitted to the hospital. Despite having flown all day, Jake drove straight from the base to his mom's bedside. He called me to share the news and asked me to meet him there.

I wasn't sure how Mr. Summers and Lucy would feel about my arrival, so I avoided the family waiting area and paced in the lobby. When Jake entered, I waited and watched. His hair lay flat against his forehead, and halos of black circled his sad eyes.

He crossed immediately to me, kissed my check, then released me and continued down the hall to find his family. I didn't follow. Instead I lowered myself into a blue polyester chair and touched my face where Jake had pressed his lips. My soul mourned because of Jake's hurt and his mom's suffering. But contentment settled in my heart. Jake's call for support, his brief kiss, signaled where we stood. The scales were balanced.

Hours passed before Jake reemerged. He found me curled up in the chair, fast asleep. I woke when he touched my shoulder.

"I can't believe you're still here," he said.

I sat up and rubbed my hands over my face. "I wanted to be here . . . for you and your mom. How is she?" I lowered my feet to the floor and stood to stretch my legs.

"She's sleeping." Jake rested his hands on his hips. "They're giving her some heavy pain meds, so she only wakes up for a few minutes before dozing off again. They're running a bunch of tests and ordered a PET scan."

"Have you been able to talk to her? Does she know you're here?" I asked.

Jake nodded and stared out the darkened window behind me. The muscles in his jaw hardened, and then he turned his eyes back to me. "She looks really fragile lying there in bed. She'd been doing better . . ."

I stepped toward him. He opened his arms, and I wrapped mine tightly around his back, pressing myself against his chest. I hoped, through the pressure of my embrace, Jake would know how much I cared about him. We held each other for a long time. I hung on tight, running my hands up and down his back while he rested his chin on my head. Eventually his hold slackened, and he wiped at his eyes.

When we leaned away from one another, his eyes were moist, and he gave me a sad smile. "Thanks," he said.

I raised my hand to his face and rubbed my thumb along the pale stubble growing on his jaw. He pressed his eyes closed, then opened them quickly and blinked several times.

"You don't have to wait out here," he said. "I know you have to work tomorrow. You can head home."

I would feel compassion for anyone in Jake's situation, but this was something more. My chest hurt for this man. A drumming ache rolled all around my heart. I cared about him, and I cared about the people who were important to him.

I took a deep breath and asked, "Do you want me to go?"

The lines in Jake's face softened. His eyes fell to mine. "No," he said.

Such a simple, loaded, honest answer.

Jake took my hand. "Come sit with us." Together we walked back to the family waiting room and sat mostly in silence until the results from Patty's test came back.

The PET scan showed the cancer had spread throughout Patty's abdomen. The acute pain was from a large tumor pressing against her stomach. The oncologist said the cancer had become inoperable and explained how Patty's time was limited. He wanted her to stay at the hospital until they found the right combination of drugs to stabilize her pain, and then they would send her home and arrange for an in-home nurse.

The family determined not to leave Patty alone. Jake took leave from work and set up a rotation with his sister and dad and insisted on taking the night shifts at the hospital, claiming he was used to the odd hours. I became the designated runner, bringing food and entertainment at varying times through the weekend. When the workweek started, I would take a nap after school, then stay up late visiting with Jake.

Patty's aversion to letting others see her pain fell away. With so many doctors and nurses coming and going, she adjusted to the rotating faces. Lucy made sure her mom's hospital room was bright and cheery, daily bringing a new assortment of fresh flowers. Patty welcomed me into her room, and when she could shake off the effect of the heavy meds enough to stay awake, she shared stories about Jake. I loved hearing her memories and watching her love for her son shine through her eyes. I bought a voice recorder and began to record her memories.

One evening I arrived as the nurse carried away a tray of hospital food. It looked like it had hardly been touched. Jake stood when I walked in, and he kissed my cheek. Patty held out her hand. I sat beside her on the bed and shared the highlight of my day; a girl I'd been working with for two years had finally mastered her ending *th* sounds.

"You are doing good work," Patty said. "I think kids don't realize how much they can accomplish if they dedicate themselves."

"I agree." I gently squeezed her hand, then moved to the chair beside Jake.

She chuckled. "Have I told you about the time I signed Jake up for tap-dancing lessons?" Patty asked.

"Oh no." Jake groaned.

Patty took a raspy breath and smiled. "He grumbled until he got to class and saw all the girls. Jake has always liked to impress." Another labored breath. "He practiced and mastered the routine. Then the instructor pulled out the costumes for the recital. Jake took one look at the bulky purple penguin outfit and refused to take the stage." Patty smiled at the memory, and Jake shook his head. I'd have to convince him to show me his dance moves sometime.

"You really didn't perform?" I asked Jake.

"Purple penguin—enough said." Jake shook his head. "A man has his pride."

With Patty's heavy dose of drugs, her waking hours were short, and she was soon asleep again.

Jake and I talked quietly. A lot. He told me about the places he'd lived growing up in the military and how the first time he'd gone to an air show with his dad, he'd known he wanted to be a pilot. He heard all about my concern for my students and my frustration with uninvolved parents, and I explained how Mandy had become my roommate.

At some point every night, the conversation turned deeper. Jake listened while I talked about my relationship with my mom. When I explained how drastically things had changed in the last few weeks, he reached over and held my hand.

"I'm glad things have improved with your mom," Jake said and glanced over at his mother, lying in peaceful sleep. "You never know when something tragic will happen."

His hold on my hand slackened, and he began playing with my fingers. We both watched his hands move over mine, caressing, lifting each finger one by one.

"She looks peaceful now," I said.

"I know." Jake sucked in a breath. "I sometimes wonder if I'm selfish to want her to live."

"Of course not," I assured him. "You love her."

"But if she's in pain, I need to let her go," he said, and sadness filled his voice.

"Jake, only God knows when it's her time to come home. You have to trust Him." I flipped my hands around and squeezed his. It had become a thing between us; I would squeeze his hand, and he would squeeze back. Only this time, his hands stilled, and he scoffed.

"What's wrong?" I asked.

"Do you really believe that?" he asked. "About God?"

"Yes. Don't you?" We'd only briefly discussed religion and our beliefs. Jake knew I attended Sunday services regularly, and while he didn't attend church, he'd told me his mom had prayed while they were growing up. He believed in God.

"Honestly, I don't know." Jake dropped my hands and ran his fingers through his hair. He watched his mother's chest rise and fall with the sound of the oxygen pump. "How could a caring God let her suffer like this?"

"Pain and trials are part of the human experience. No one is exempt from suffering." The routine words came automatically, but the explanation felt cheap. I took a long breath, then another, and I prayed for guidance to better convey how I felt. "I don't know why some have a harder path," I whispered. "I only know God knows us. He loves us."

"Loves us?" Jake stood and held his hand toward the hospital bed, where his mother lay in a drug-induced sleep. "My mom is a good woman. She's lived a good life, raised responsible children, and supported her husband and been faithful to him. She doesn't deserve this."

I didn't have an answer. I only had my faith. "Have you prayed to ask for comfort? Comfort for your mom and peace for you?"

Jake's hands dropped to his side. His fingers curled into fists. His voice was low, resigned. "I don't know that I can pray to a God who allows good people to suffer."

Several more canned adages came to mind: *Without the pain, we can't know the good. Our pain cannot compare to Christ's suffering. Trials make us stronger.*

Each had merit. Each held truth. But none of them felt right. Jake was hurt and angry. He was confused. But blaming God was not the answer. A thought came to mind. "We don't know all that God knows, but I believe He is fair and just. He has a plan for your mom, and I believe that plan includes her receiving all the joy she deserves. It may just come on a timeline that's different from what you imagined."

Jake walked to his mother's side and stroked her hair from her forehead.

"Take every opportunity you have to tell her how much you love her. Make sure she knows how you feel, and it will be enough," I said.

"What other choice do I have?" Jake asked. "She's slipping away, and no amount of prayer is going to change that."

CHAPTER 17
I Discovered (Eureka!)

THE DOCTORS SENT PATTY HOME on Friday. Her time in the hospital left her weak and confined to a wheelchair. An in-home nurse was scheduled to come every evening to monitor Patty's medications and sit with her through the night. Lucy hired additional help at the flower shop in order to spend more time with her mother during the day, and Jake drove down every evening after work.

Mr. Summers's military benefits provided excellent care for his wife. Once Patty moved home, her spirits improved. She still took frequent naps, but she also smiled more. She was a living example of the glass-is-half-full outlook. Despite her discomfort and uncertain future, she found joy in simple things. Jake and his family remained in my prayers. Patty's prognosis was not good, but I prayed that if it was God's will, he would grant a miracle.

On Patty's third day home, I got a call from Jake. "Are you going to your family dinner today?" he asked.

I wasn't sure what answer he wanted, so I tried to cover all the bases in my response. "I thought your family would want some time alone, so yeah, I was going to head to my parents'." I paused, then said, "But I can change things around if you need me to."

"No, I actually hoped to ask your mom for a favor," Jake said.

"Okay." I laughed, suddenly curious. "What's up?"

"My mom's asking for something sweet, and I know she loved those cookies your mom sent. Do you know if she's made any lately?"

This was a wish I could grant. "My mom is a cookie master. If she doesn't have any on hand, she can whip them up pretty quickly."

"You don't think it would be a problem?" Jake asked.

"Jake, you're talking about a woman who would rather run out of toilet paper than chocolate chips. Trust me; it's no problem."

"Thanks, Paige. You're the best," he said.

"We'll give my mom the credit on this one," I said.

"Tell her she's pretty cool too."

"Deal. I'll bring them by later."

As I expected, Mom had no qualms about whipping up a batch of cookies. When I arrived for dinner, she had finished the dough and was ready to start baking.

"Can you scoop the cookies?" Mom asked.

I wasn't the best baker, but I could do the manual labor. I washed my hands and began working next to Mom. She stirred a pot of soup on the stove and told me she'd doubled the recipe so I could take some to Jake's family.

"It's always nice to have an easy meal in the fridge," Mom said. "I figured I'd send some rolls as well."

I placed another scoop of cookie dough onto the pan, set down the spoon, then walked behind my mom and wrapped my arms around her. "Thanks, Mom." I planned to say more, to tell Mom how much her gesture meant, but I got choked up and stood there, silently blinking back my emotions.

Mom didn't speak either. She let the spoon drop against the side of the pot and raised her arms to wrap them around mine.

In that moment the shroud of anger lifted from my eyes. The eureka moment was not one I'd expected, and it hit me like a brick wall. Mom meddled because of her love for us. She may not always take the best approach, but I discovered that her intentions were pure. She wanted to know the details of our lives in order to take care of us. I'd been holding back for years, assuming that if I didn't share, she would take the hint and let me live my life. I think she always intended to let me figure out things on my own, and in my efforts to push her away, she'd pushed back just as hard. She couldn't let me go, not knowing whether I would be ready for reality. When I opened up and shared with her, she stepped back and offered assistance when I needed it. Even when I didn't expect it, she saw the need and helped quietly. Mom needed reassurance, and my efforts to detach had ended up being counterproductive.

I squeezed Mom tight and then let go and moved back to finish scooping cookie dough.

Everyone asked about Jake and his family, and after I shared an update on Patty, dinner became a quiet affair. Amelia, Max, and Nathaniel claimed most of the attention and kept us entertained. Their spinning minds and curious questions reminded me of the beauty of life. I knew peace and love existed amid turmoil. The joy accompanying those feelings made the journey worth enduring. I believed in God's promises. Great blessings were in store when we endured.

Jake's mother was sleeping when I arrived. His father accepted the soup gratefully, and his eyes moistened when I handed him a dozen of Mom's homemade rolls. The food probably served as a reminder of all the things Patty had provided when her body was whole. Jake took the cookies and snuck one before placing the remainder of the plate near his mom's bed.

He told me it had been a hard day. The pain had been intense, but Patty insisted she could handle it. She didn't want to be medicated and unable to remember the time she had left with her family.

Jake's eyes bore the marks of his exhaustion. "Once the sun set, she determined the day was over and finally allowed the nurse to give her the meds," Jake said. "I can't stand to see her in so much pain."

"She's okay now," I tried to assure him. "You need to sleep while she does. Rest so you can be available for her tomorrow."

Jake nodded and walked me to the door. "Thank you, Paige. This means a lot to my mom, but it also means a lot to me." I offered him a small smile. "Please tell your mom how grateful we are," he said.

"I think she knows," I said. "But I'll tell her."

He gave me a single kiss good night, and I left.

When I walked through my door, I felt different. My concerns weighed heavily, but for the first time I felt that perhaps I could handle the burden because I'd realized I could share it not only with God but with my mom. My epiphany about my mother seemed simple. The truth had loomed all around me, waiting for me to understand it. I wondered why it had taken me so long.

Mandy knew something had changed. I told her about my day and the revelation I'd had about my mother's interference.

"I don't know why I didn't realize before," I said.

"I guess now that you point it out, it does seem obvious." Mandy shrugged. "But at the time you couldn't see past the fact that it bothered you."

"True," I said.

"How's Jake holding up?" Mandy asked.

Mandy knew firsthand how hard it was to watch someone suffer. Last year her grandmother had died of cancer after having fought a long, painful battle. I remember Mandy telling me the worst thing was wanting the person to fight despite knowing the cancer would win in the end. Some cancers can be beat, but the lymphoma her grandmother had contracted was fatal. When she saw her grandmother's determination to battle, Mandy couldn't concede defeat. Jake, too, refused to give up.

"You know how tough it is," I told Mandy.

I set down my stuff, and she came over and squeezed my shoulder. "How are you?"

I shrugged and slumped into a kitchen chair. "Holding up." I faked a smile and conjured up some enthusiasm. "Tell me how your plans are coming. Brandon gets back this week!" I clapped my hands in excitement, anxious to talk about a happy event.

Jake hadn't asked for my time, but I'd given him a lot of it lately. Mandy's wedding was two weeks away, and I determined to celebrate my best friend's moment to the fullest.

"Brandon's internship is over on Wednesday, and he's driving back Thursday," she said. "Paige . . ." She looked at me, and her eyes sparkled. "He got the job."

Brandon had interviewed with a firm in San Francisco. After Mandy moved out, I planned to stay in our rental house through the end of the school year, then reevaluate. I knew my life would change when Mandy got married. I knew things would be different. But when she told me San Francisco might be a possibility, I got excited. Brandon would commute while Mandy finished up the school year. In a few months they would move away, but I could handle driving an hour or two to see Mandy. It was the best-case scenario, considering Brandon had also interviewed in New York.

"Wow! That's huge. Is it the one he really wants? I mean, the one you both want?" I couldn't contain the selfish excitement I felt. "Is he going to take it?"

When I looked back up at Mandy, I knew the decision had been made. She'd be able to stay close to her family and still hang with me once the newlywed bliss wore off.

I grinned, not hiding the contentment I felt. "I'm happy for you, Mandy. Brandon too. You deserve this, and San Francisco is much better than New York. Hopefully, you and Prince Charming will be able to spare some time for your old roomie," I teased.

"Your time will come, Paige," she said. "Don't give up. Darcy's out there somewhere."

"Yeah, with his white horse and breeches," I said with a light laugh.

"Maybe he has blue eyes and flies airplanes." Mandy pushed up from the table with a wink as she said, "Don't forget you need a date for the wedding."

I hadn't forgotten.

CHAPTER 18
I Asked

NOT MUCH CHANGED IN THE following days. I tried to give Jake's family space and only stopped by for brief visits. I used the evenings to finalize plans for Mandy's bridal shower. She wanted only a few close friends and her mother invited, so I'd booked a room at a quaint restaurant at a nearby lake. The large windows looking over the lake negated the need for any decor. The menu was solidified, and all that remained were the favors for the guests and a gift for Mandy. I'd pondered for more than a month about what to get her. I wanted something sentimental, something more than a Crock-Pot or a scented candle.

Midway through the week, Mom called to tell me she had made her famous spaghetti, homemade breadsticks, a salad, and brownies for the Summerses. I texted Jake, telling him I would bring dinner, and went by my parents' house after work.

"Smells delicious," I told my mom.

She stood at the counter, adding creamy frosting to the brownies. "Want one?" she asked.

"No, I need to fit into my dress for the wedding, and I'm counting down the days." I kissed her cheek.

"You'll look great." Mom made a final swirl on the top of the frosting and carried her spatula and bowl to the sink. She turned around and put one hand on her hip. "Did you ask Jake to go with you yet?"

I grimaced and immediately put up a wall. Then I looked at Mom again and saw the sincerity of her question. I took a breath, then answered, "There hasn't been a good time to bring it up. It doesn't seem right to talk about dressing fancy and dancing at Mandy's happily-ever-after when he's surrounded by such sorrow."

Mom walked over and placed her hand over mine. I looked up into her eyes. "Maybe a little happily-ever-after is what Jake needs right now. There's never a wrong time to feel happy."

"You think so?" I asked.

"I do. Ask him." She tilted her head. "Let Jake determine what he needs."

"What if he says no? I mean, I don't think he would if he weren't going through this, but it might be too much, and I don't want to go with anyone else," I said.

"I'll lend you your father for the night." Mom winked. "He's a great-looking guy and a pretty good dancer."

I smiled. "Thanks, Mom."

We loaded my car with the dinner and brownies, and I drove to the Summerses' house. After carrying everything in, Jake led me to his mother's room to say hello.

Patty sat in bed with half a dozen pillows propped around her.

"Hey," I said with a smile. The past few days she'd been sleeping when I had stopped by. "You look great." I walked over and sat in a chair near her bed.

She didn't answer, but she raised her hand toward me. I scooted to the edge of my chair, and when I placed my hand in hers, she closed her fingers around mine.

"Paige brought spaghetti and brownies for dinner, Mom," Jake said from where he stood behind me.

"I don't know how my mom's brownies will compare to yours, but chocolate is chocolate, right?" I gently squeezed Patty's hand.

Her lips turned up in a small smile, and when she spoke, her voice was barely a whisper. "You be good to my Jake."

I looked over my shoulder at Jake. His face pulled tight with worry. I didn't know what to say to Patty. How did she expect me to respond? I wanted so badly to do right by both of them, yet I knew any words I uttered would be wrong.

I felt the smallest pull on my hand and turned back around to Patty. "He'll be good to you," she said. Then she drew in a labored breath.

The words came to me then, and their truth warmed me as I spoke. "You've raised a good man, Patty."

"I know," she said. Then she turned her head to the side and closed her eyes.

I watched her chest rise and fall until I knew she'd fallen asleep. I stood and lowered her hand to rest on the bed and followed Jake from the room.

In the hallway Jake stopped and turned back toward me. Without a word he pulled me into his arms. He held me firmly and buried his head in my hair.

"Thank you," he whispered.

I stood there, content to let him hold on as long as he needed to. I closed my eyes and savored the feeling of his strong arms embracing me. His warmth spread through me, and the sensation feathered out to my limbs. He smelled like soap and a touch of fragrant aftershave.

When he finally stepped back, he gave me a rueful smile. I reached my hand to touch his cheek. "I meant what I said. You're a good man."

He leaned forward and kissed my cheek, then took my hand and led me to the kitchen. Four place settings sat at the counter.

"You'll join us, won't you, Paige?" Mr. Summers asked.

"Of course she will," Lucy chimed in. "We need to talk wedding details."

I stiffened until my brain made the connection that she was talking about Mandy's wedding. I agreed to stay, and during the meal Lucy gave me the rundown on the arrangements.

"Thank you for recommending me," Lucy said.

"I can't take the credit. After the stargazer lilies arrived, Mandy was sold," I said. "You should thank your brother."

"Well, it's taken him long enough to cash in on the discount I give him. It's about time he sent flowers to someone." She turned toward Jake and gave him a curt nod.

Jake shook his head and took another bite. Mr. Summers silently watched the interaction during dinner. He didn't say much, and I assumed his mind weighed heavily with thoughts of Patty.

When we finished, Lucy sent him away. "Go sit with Mom. We've got this."

Mr. Summers set his napkin on his plate and disappeared down the hall. I offered to load the dishwasher while Lucy and Jake cleared the dishes and stored the leftovers. Lucy carried most of the conversation, asking continual questions about Mandy's wedding.

"Have you ever been to Dunlap Gardens?" she asked me.

I shook my head.

"I've only been once, and it was for a night wedding. The place was beautiful," she said with emphasis. "Hundreds of twinkle lights hung around the gazebo, and paper lanterns were strung over the lawn and dance floor." She sighed and grabbed a rag to wipe off the counter.

"Mandy wants to keep it small, and she planned the time so they'll be married right before sunset," I said.

"Oh . . ." Lucy moaned. "It sounds divine."

"At least, the flowers will be perfect," Jake said.

Lucy and I looked at each other and laughed.

"What?" Jake's eyes widened.

"I like how you felt the need to comment so you weren't completely left out of the conversation," Lucy teased.

I put the last plate into the dishwasher.

"All I'm saying is that if you're doing them, they'll be great." He moved the pan of brownies near the fridge.

"Of course they will be," Lucy said and smiled at me. She returned the rag to the sink and washed off her hands. "You're a bridesmaid, right?"

"Maid of honor." I smiled.

"Oh, even better," Lucy said. "What does your dress look like?"

Certainly, Jake didn't need details, but Lucy deserved to have a moment of levity. I described the tea-length coral dress Mandy had chosen, from the pleated wrapped bodice to the flared twirl skirt. Every last detail.

Lucy leaned against the counter with her chin in one hand. "I can't wait to see it. You'll definitely show up your date." Lucy pumped her eyebrows, then looked at her brother, who leaned against the counter.

My breath froze in my chest. "Actually—" I licked my lips and turned to look at Jake. "Do you want to go for a walk?" Lucy had given me the perfect opening.

Lucy looked between us, and I think she realized we hadn't talked about going to the wedding. "I'll go check on Dad. Nurse Jenny will be here soon," she said and made a quick exit.

Nerves suddenly swam through my chest. I knew if Jake accompanied me, it would be a sacrifice of his time, and for Jake, time was a precious commodity. Mandy's wedding was important to me, and I wanted Jake by my side. His mother needed him, but I needed him too.

Since Lucy had left, there was no reason for us to go into the chilly night air. I took a breath and jumped in. "So you know Mandy's wedding is in two weeks, and I wondered if you might want to go with me."

"As your plus one?" Jake asked with a teasing grin.

"Something like that," I said and smiled back.

He reached out his hand, and I stepped forward to take it.

"As in, I would get to escort the most beautiful woman there?" He took a step toward me and lifted my hand to his lips. After a soft kiss on my knuckles, he looked down at me through his lashes.

My breath hitched in my throat. After a few moments, I said, "Well, the bride should be the most beautiful, and Mandy already has a date—the groom, actually."

Jake shook his head. "Oh, I wasn't talking about Mandy."

The sultry tone in his voice took me by surprise. I hadn't seen this side of Jake before. I liked his mischievous flirting.

He pushed my hair back from my face and brought his lips to mine. Elation surged through me at the surety of his movement. It lasted for only a moment, but my equilibrium faltered.

Jake stepped back, leaving one hand on my waist. "I'd love to go with you," he said, but as quickly as I inhaled my delight, the moment shifted. "Unless . . . of course . . ." His eyes flicked to the hallway leading to his mother.

"Of course, yeah." I stepped back. The warmth of his kiss still burned on my lips. "I should be going." I located my purse and jacket, and Jake walked me to the door.

We said good night, and before I drove away, I sent a text to my mother telling her dinner was delicious, that I'd finally asked Jake, and he'd said yes.

CHAPTER 19
I Mourned

I DIDN'T SEE JAKE UNTIL the following Tuesday. Patty's condition had worsened, and Nurse Jenny now stayed at the house full time. I knew things were bad when Jake sent a quick text telling me he didn't go in to work. Armed with Mom's banana bread, I stopped by for a quick visit.

Jake welcomed me with tired eyes and a long hug. "Wanna say hi to my mom?" he asked.

"I don't want to impose," I said.

"Come on," Jake said and motioned for me to follow him.

We stepped inside the room while Nurse Jenny scribbled numbers down from one of Patty's new monitors. The machines beeped, and Patty's chest rose and fell slowly as she lay in peaceful sleep.

"She's slipping away," Jake said, and his breath caught.

I placed my hand in his, and we both stared at his mother's frail body. Her fight had left her weak. Her cheeks were sallow, her lips thin and pale. At least in sleep she couldn't feel pain.

But Jake could.

I wanted to take away his misery. To tell him everything would be okay, but that would be a lie, and I'd promised him honesty. The truth was he would hurt. Patty's passing would be hard. Comfort was available through God's love and the peace Christ provided, but Jake would have to accept their divine offering. He would have to trust in God's plan for his mother. For him.

We stood in silence until Mr. Summers returned to his bedside chair. Jake blinked his eyes clear. "I'll bring you both some dinner," he said to his dad and the nurse.

I placed my hand on Mr. Summers's shoulder as we left the room. Jake stopped in the front hall.

"I'll go," I said and took a step toward the front door. I hesitantly turned back. "Unless you want some help . . . or some company?"

"No," Jake said quickly, and although I didn't mean to, I jerked back in response. Jake sighed and rubbed a hand over his face. "I mean, thank you, but no. Lucy should be home any minute."

"Okay," I said with a small smile. I pulled my keys from my purse, offered my goodbye, and walked out the door.

The next day as I pulled into a parking spot at my school, I got a text from Jake. *Mom passed last night. I'll call you in a few days.*

My heart mourned. Although I hadn't known Patty long, I knew she was a beautiful person. She'd welcomed me into her home and into her son's life. I wanted to call Jake. I wanted to hold him. But nothing I could do would provide the solace he needed.

Mandy suggested sending flowers. Heather said I should give him time. Neither of those things felt right. I responded to his text with a simple *I'm so sorry*, knowing how insufficient the words sounded.

I called my mom and told her what had happened.

"Oh, Paige, I continue to pray for their family," Mom said. "This has to be so tough for them."

"I don't know what to say or do. Jake and I haven't exactly had a define-the-relationship talk. I want to do something, but I'm at a loss," I confessed.

"What does your heart tell you?" Mom asked.

I moaned. "I don't know. I guess I'm sad because I know Jake is sad. I can't say, 'She's in a better place' or, 'At least she's not hurting anymore,' because those words sound hollow. I know the family needs time to mourn, but I feel helpless."

Mom stayed silent.

"Mom?" I asked.

I heard her sigh. "You won't like what I'm going to say."

I leaned my head back on the couch. "Out with it," I said.

"I think Jake told you exactly what he needed with his text," she said. "I know it's hard because you want to do more, but all he's asking you for right now is patience and time."

"Okay," I said. "I can give him that."

"It would be nice to send a sympathy card to the family, but just drop it in the mail. Then find something to keep you busy so you don't go crazy wondering when Jake will call," Mom said. She knew me well. "And pray for him."

"So a card, patience, and prayer?" I repeated.

"Yes. At least, that's my advice," Mom said. "I'd like to send a card as well. Please text me his address when you get a chance."

Mom's counsel left me deflated. I was ready to move forward in my relationship with Jake. I liked him a lot, but the fear that I would mess things up added a layer of complication to every decision. My pledge for spontaneity vanished, and I resigned myself to patience.

When I told Mandy Mom's advice, she listened quietly and then nodded in agreement. "She's right," she said. "After my grandma died, so many people stopped in to see Grandpa. It was tiring and prolonged his grieving. We finally convinced him to go stay with my parents in Arizona for a few months. He needed a break, a change of scenery."

"Well, I'm going to do what Jake asked and stay away for a while." I slapped my hands down on my lap. "In fact, I know just the thing to distract me." I stood and grabbed my purse. "I have a shower gift to buy."

Mandy wagged her finger at me. "You don't have to buy anything, Paige. Throwing the shower is gift enough."

I opened my eyes wide, planted one hand on my hip, and attempted to give Mandy my teacher's glare. "Are you trying to test my patience already?"

"You know what I'm saying," Mandy said.

"Yes, and I know I need to keep busy." I snatched my keys from the counter and hooked my purse over my shoulder. "Don't wait up," I said and smiled as I walked out to my car.

But as soon as I pulled out of the driveway, my smile vanished. Mandy was my best friend, and I'd known her way longer than Jake. She needed to know his problems didn't change my devotion to her. This wedding was her dream, and I wanted her to know of my happiness for her, but this was another situation in which words seemed inadequate. I needed to find the perfect gift—the kind for which words weren't needed. I determined to keep my mind focused on my mission.

After I wandered through multiple boutiques and home-goods stores, my patience was stretched as thin as my culinary skills. I stopped by Millie's and ordered a caramel cinnamon hot chocolate.

As I sipped the warm heavenly goodness, I scrolled back to Jake's text. He hadn't responded to me, so I read again, *Mom passed last night. I'll call you in a few days.* I hoped *few* would lean toward the shorter end of things, then felt completely selfish for thinking of how much I wanted to see him.

I wanted him to need me. Only God could provide absolute peace. Only God could heal Jake's heart. But Jake had become a staple in my life. I wanted to be an anchor for him. I wanted to pray with him, to work through trials by his side, to let him know he could lean on me. Because one thing I'd realized in the past month was that I needed him.

CHAPTER 20
I partied

After four days, I still hadn't heard from Jake. I'd sent a card like Mom had advised and was certain it had arrived, but still—nothing. My determination to be happy for Mandy brewed stronger than ever. I pumped her up for her bridal shower and racked my brain for a gift. Mandy wasn't picky, but since I wanted my present to have meaning, I put a lot of thought and energy into coming up with something great. By week's end I was no closer to finding a gift, and Jake's continued silence made it imperative for me to keep my focus on the party.

At my family dinner, everyone expressed their condolences, which seemed strange since I obviously had no tangible connection to the Summers, but I accepted their offering and changed the subject.

Heather asked all sorts of questions about Mandy's wedding. She agreed to come help style my hair and makeup before the ceremony. I gave her details about the flowers, the dresses, the food, and the music.

"It sounds like a great venue. Maybe one day you'll get married there," Heather said.

"I'd need a fiancé for that," I said sarcastically and made a face, daring my sister to disagree.

As the older sister, Heather had the gumption to ignore my sarcasm. "Which is why a wedding is the perfect place to take a guy you're serious about. It puts ideas into his head."

I faked a smile and turned away from Heather to watch Amelia and Max play with Matt's old toy cars.

"Paige?" Heather prodded. "What's wrong?"

"Nothing," I lied, glancing at her briefly before turning back to the kids.

"Yeah right," she said. "What's up?"

"I, uh . . . haven't heard from Jake. I'm trying to give him space and be respectful, but it's hard. I'm not sure he'll make it to the wedding." It felt good to confess my fears to Heather. She'd always proved to be a good listener.

"It's still a week away. I'm sure you'll talk to him by then," she said and tried to offer a bona fide smile.

"I saw in the paper that the funeral service is Wednesday," I said, then let out a derisive laugh. "Jake didn't even tell me."

Mom stood from where she'd been visiting with the men and moved to sit by us. "Are we talking about Jake?" she asked.

Heather looked at me, then filled Mom in. "Paige knows the funeral is on Wednesday because she saw it in the paper, but Jake still hasn't called."

"It takes a lot of time to plan for burial arrangements. Jake's probably taken the lead and been swamped. I'm sure he wanted to tell you," Mom said.

I looked sideways at her. "If he wanted me at the service, I think he would've found thirty seconds to send a text with the details."

"You said he doesn't like to text," Mom said.

"He doesn't, but ironically that's how he told me about his mom passing, and that's the last time I heard from him." Max threw a car, and it hit my leg. I bent over and picked it up.

"Maybe he lost his phone." Heather held her palms up and made a convincing face, but I frowned to let her know I wasn't sold.

"Really?" I asked. "It's okay," I lied and stood up. "I'll decide if I should take the day off and go to the funeral . . . or not." I shrugged.

Mom stood next to me and pulled me into a side hug. "If you decide you want company, I'd be happy to go with you."

"I know he'll be busy at the service, and I'm not expecting much. I'm also concerned about the wedding. I don't know if I should offer him an out or wait and see what happens. I mean, it won't be a big deal if I don't have a date, right?"

"Remember, I said you could have Dad for the night?" Mom smiled. "He won't mind being a last-minute standby."

"What would Elizabeth Bennet do? Or better yet, what would Mr. Darcy do?" Heather asked with a wide smile. "This could be a defining moment for Jake. I mean, every girl loves when her hero rushes in to save her. Mandy will be living her happily ever after, which leaves you to be the damsel in distress."

I scoffed at Heather's theatrics. "I'm not a damsel in distress, but you did just give me a great idea for Mandy's shower gift—a huge basket loaded with all things Jane Austen. Mandy's been relying on my stock all these years. It's time she got her own."

I offered my first sincere smile of the week. It didn't last long though. One problem down. One to go.

By the time I got home after work on Tuesday, I was a mess. I hadn't left as early as I had planned because I'd decided to attend Patty's funeral the next morning, which meant notifying the teachers, along with all of my students, to remain in class rather than come to speech. Mandy's shower started in exactly one hour, and it would take thirty minutes to get there.

I scuttled through the front door and put on a happy smile. Light glowed from under Mandy's bedroom door. "Hey, Mandy," I called down the hallway in an extremely chipper voice. "I'll be ready to go in twenty."

I hated feeling frazzled and was grateful I had Mandy's present wrapped and stashed in my trunk. Mom had gone on a Jane Austen hunt while I was at work on Monday. She'd found everything on the list I'd provided except the long Colin Firth version of *Pride and Prejudice*. Of course, that item was a must, so I'd bequeathed mine to Mandy's gift basket and had already ordered a replacement online. Mom had also thought to include an assortment of tea, chocolates, candles, and a gift certificate to a specialty bakery that made pastries. I owed Mom. Big time. The basket burst with Regency flair, and I was quite pleased with the end result.

I changed out of my work clothes and slipped on a simple eggplant-colored cocktail dress. There was no time to do my hair, so I twisted the sides back into a low ponytail and then added fresh lip gloss and mascara. I hopped out the door while slipping on my black pumps and called for Mandy.

Once we were on the road, my heartbeat settled. We chatted easily, and when Mandy asked about Jake, I told her I was going to attend the funeral in the morning and changed the subject.

The room I'd reserved was in perfect order, and our small group chatted, laughed, and devoured the delicious food. I tortured Mandy with only one bridal game, pitting her memory against Brandon's. I asked Mandy questions about their first date, first kiss, and Brandon's favorite song. She answered, and I shared Brandon's responses to the same questions. I watched in amazement as Mandy answered nearly every question identically to Brandon. They really were a perfect match. The only question Mandy missed was when I asked which laundry detergent Brandon preferred. Mandy blamed her miss on the fact that they hadn't done laundry together.

"Ask me again next week," Mandy said with a grin. "No, actually, you'd better wait until after the honeymoon."

The conversation then switched to the trip to Orlando Brandon had planned. I knew all the details and sat contently listening to Mandy explain the specifics of their eight-day and seven-night trip filled with marital honeymoon bliss. Mandy's eyes lit with excitement, and my heart swelled for my friend.

We stayed until almost eleven. I was tired but wanted desperately to hold on to this last memory with Mandy. In only four days I would arrive home to an empty house.

The waiter from the restaurant helped us load all of Mandy's gifts into my car. She loved the Jane Austen basket and had almost cried when she saw I had passed on my well-worn DVD to her. The other guests didn't quite understand the sentimentality, but they also didn't know how many times Mandy and I had sat through marathon viewings of *Pride and Prejudice*. We could recite Elizabeth Bennet's monologues with convincing passion.

As we started the drive home, Mandy thanked me for the wonderful shower.

I glanced at her and smiled. "You're welcome."

"Promise when your time comes, I get to host yours," Mandy said.

"*If* my time comes, it's all you," I answered, though she may have to arm wrestle my sister.

Mandy scoffed. "If . . . whatever!"

We drove the next few miles in silence. I didn't doubt I would get married someday, but looking at Mandy, I knew I wouldn't settle for anything less than absolute bliss.

"How did you know?" I asked, staring ahead at the dark road.

"What?" Mandy asked.

"How did you know Brandon would make you happy for the rest of your life?"

Mandy mulled it over. She lifted her left hand off her lap and fiddled with her engagement ring. "I guess one day I realized Brandon was different from other guys I had dated." She took a breath and sighed in a swoony sort of way. "I couldn't imagine my life without Brandon in it, and when he told me he felt the same, suddenly everything was okay."

"What do you mean?" I asked.

"You remember how we were always together?"

"Yeah," I said with a laugh.

"It's because we were afraid to be apart, like if we weren't physically seeing one another, something might happen to break the connection." Mandy shook her head. "I don't know if I'm making sense." She shifted and folded one leg up on her seat as she turned to face me. "I guess I didn't trust Brandon at first. I mean, I trusted him, but I didn't trust that his feelings were as strong as mine. Once he told me how he felt, we talked about a future together, and something clicked. I didn't worry about where we stood anymore because my heart told me we were in love. I trusted Brandon, and it was okay to be away from him because I knew he missed me as much as I missed him." She shrugged. "Somehow I just knew it. I guess that's why the internship didn't pull us apart."

"It didn't," I agreed. "In fact, you seem closer than ever."

"Which is a good thing since we're getting married on Saturday." Mandy's cheeks pulled up in a smile.

"Lucky girl," I said.

"Yes. I. Am." Mandy turned forward and grinned the rest of the way home.

We unloaded the car, and I dropped into bed just after midnight. I picked up my phone to set my alarm, and on the screen I saw a text from Jake. *I know it's late, but I wanted to tell you Mom's service is tomorrow at ten, Kensington Memorial Chapel.*

"I'll be there," I said to myself. Then I fell asleep.

CHAPTER 21
I Grieved (with Gratitude)

MOM AND I ARRIVED EARLY. The doors to the chapel were still closed. Guests lingered in the foyer, and my nerves rattled on overdrive. My eyes constantly scanned the room for a familiar face, while my ears jumbled the whispered conversations through my head.

I wore a simple black pencil skirt with a pale-pink blouse and clutched my small purse until my knuckles turned white.

Mom leaned toward me and whispered, "They're probably meeting with the family and finalizing everything before they open the doors to the guests."

I nodded agreement, and when my eyes swept the room again I saw a man in a black suit stepping toward us.

"Welcome," he said. "Are you family or friends of the family?"

"Friends," I said.

"Okay. When you enter, you'll notice the first four rows have been reserved for family. Feel free to find a seat behind the reserved section," he said.

I nodded, and he shook my hand in unison with the groaning of the heavy wooden doors as they opened. The guests quieted and made their way inside. As Mom and I moved with the mass, I noticed a portrait of Patty on an easel near the door. I paused for a moment to look at the picture of a younger Patty. Jake had inherited his mother's eyes, and in the simplicity of Patty's smile, I could sense her happiness, her joy for life. I grieved that her time had passed, but I was grateful I was able to know her, even if it was only for a short time.

Mom stood silently beside me, and people continued to arrive, but the larger crowd had cleared the lobby. I turned to follow a couple in and saw Lucy and her father greeting guests at the door.

"Paige!" Lucy said and pulled me into a hug. "I'm so glad to see you."

I quickly wrapped my arms around her, surprised at her enthusiastic greeting. Mr. Summers stood next to her, dressed in full military uniform, and although his expression was somber, he lifted his mouth in a small smile. I introduced them both to my mother, and we turned to find a seat.

Mom moved down the aisle, but as I followed, Lucy grabbed my arm and pulled me back. "Have you seen Jake yet?" she asked, and I shook my head. Her smile instantly faded. Her eyes closed, and she bowed her head. "He's a mess," she said and looked back up at me, her face full of sorrow. "He seemed composed the whole time Mom was sick, but once she passed . . . He's taking it hard. It's like he's pulled into a shell."

A new kind of sadness filled me. "He asked me to give him time—"

"No, I didn't mean for you . . ." Lucy shook her head and exhaled. "I just wanted you to know."

I bit my lip and thought about what Lucy had revealed. Her father called her attention to an older gentleman, and I walked numbly to where my mother sat.

A pianist played through a medley of songs as guests continued to file in, and my mind absorbed the music, swaying my thoughts with the airy notes. I'd assumed Jake hadn't called me because he was busy, and while I hadn't told anyone, I'd inwardly blamed him for not taking time. Now I realized I'd been selfish to think I'd played any role in his actions. I'd been focused on myself and my insecurities about where we stood rather than considering how Jake was holding up.

The Jake I knew exuded confidence. His military persona was assertive and strong, not the type to pull away when his family needed him. Should I have called him? Would I have been able to help, or was I again placing too much emphasis on my importance? The comfort I could offer would only go so far. I wasn't what Jake needed. He needed God. Jake needed to surrender his sorrow and his confusion to Deity. It was the only way he would find peace.

The clock neared ten, and the pianist played a final chord. Lucy and her father walked to their seats on the front pew. Jake emerged from a side entrance and joined them. His military attire matched his father's and made him appear regal and sturdy, yet in the small glimpse I got of his face, I knew it was an illusion.

A man stood at the podium, and we all bowed our heads as he offered an invocation. Various relatives assisted in the program, and as stories and memories were shared, the joy Patty had found in life filled the chapel. I hoped when my time on Earth ended, I would be remembered as fondly.

Near the end of the service, Lucy stood and thanked everyone for their support. She shared a brief memory of her mother, wiped the tears from her eyes, and at the conclusion looked toward Jake. Her hopeful expression served as an invitation for him to stand and say a few words.

The moment stretched long, and I knew Lucy's concerns for her brother were valid. Jake didn't shy away from a challenge. He met situations head-on. I'd witnessed his strength time and again. First, when he'd approached me in the parking lot, insistent on making amends, and then when he and his family had told me how he'd earned his call sign by standing up to his superiors. Jake's kindness had manifested at the career fair and again as he'd cared for his mother. As I'd gotten to know him, I'd never doubted his goodness or his strength. What held him back now?

The crowd waited patiently for a glimpse of Patty's resilience to manifest through her son. Couldn't Jake feel it? Then he shifted and stood. I exhaled, and my heart lifted. There was the dauntless man I knew.

Jake made his way to the front and turned slowly to face the crowd. He braced his hands on either side of the podium and stared silently at the base of the microphone. "Patricia Summers, my mom, was an amazing lady. She expected the best from people, and those expectations kept me out of a lot of trouble. When I was in high school, every time I left the house, Mom would say, 'Go change the world.'" Jake took a shaky breath, then looked up at his dad. "Those words and the fear that somehow I would disappoint my mother helped me make good choices, right choices. I always wanted to come home better than how I left. The person I am today is entirely due to my mom, and I hope one day I can inspire someone the way she has inspired me." Jake's eyes darted to the closed coffin. "I love you, Mom," he said, his voice laced with emotion. Then he returned to his seat.

I wiped at my eyes, and when Mom handed me a tissue, I saw that she was crying too. My heart swelled at Jake's courage to stand in tribute to his mother. I couldn't find my voice, and instead of joining in, I listened to the rest of the congregation sing a final song, and then the benediction was offered. Jake and his father led a procession of family and uniformed military out a side door, and the guests followed. The pallbearers lifted Patty's coffin into the hearse, and once the doors were closed, hugs were given, and the mourners began to disperse, except for the family.

Mom put a hand on my shoulder. "What do you want to do?" she asked.

I lifted my chin and tried to dredge up some bravery. "I think I should say hello."

Mom's eyes brightened. She rubbed my shoulder and nodded. "I'll wait here," she said.

Jake stood talking to an older man dressed in military attire. I stopped a few feet away, but the conversation ended, and both men looked at me expectantly.

"I'm sorry. I didn't mean to interrupt," I said as the butterflies in my stomach began a game of tug-of-war.

"Uh . . ." Jake said, and he looked between me and the other gentleman. "Paige, this is Colonel Halton; he's my group commander." Jake's arm swung toward me. "Sir, this is Paige Hall . . . a family friend."

While Jake and I had never had the relationship talk, I knew I wanted to be acknowledged as more than "a family friend." One side had just gained some major ground in the tug-of-war, and my fragile heart balanced on a precarious ledge as I wondered if it would soon be a casualty of the game.

Colonel Halton extended his hand, and I shook it. "It's a pleasure to meet you, Miss Hall," the Colonel said. Then he looked back at Jake. "Take the rest of the week off, and we'll touch base on Monday."

"Thank you, sir. I appreciate you coming," Jake said. Then he lifted his right hand in a salute, and Colonel Halton returned the gesture before walking away.

Jake watched Colonel Halton's back for a long minute before turning to acknowledge me. When he did turn around, his eyes were steely and distant.

"Thanks for coming," he said acerbically.

My lungs felt like they had collapsed. "I . . . I wanted to come. I realize I didn't know your mother for very long, but she was kind to me. Her positive attitude was contagious," I said, offering a hopeful smile.

When Jake didn't answer, I looked back up to his face. Muscles clenched his jaw tight, and his eyes were trained on something over my shoulder. I turned around and saw Lucy standing across the parking lot. She stared at us, and I recalled her words from earlier. She had warned me Jake was depressed. Patty's passing had hit him deeply, stealing his normal, easygoing vivacity. I had hoped, when he stood during the funeral, he would find closure, but peace seemed to elude him.

I turned back to face him, and he said, "Thanks again for coming." Then he took a step to move past me.

"Jake, wait," I said and touched his arm. He stiffened and stopped walking. "I'm sorry for your loss," I whispered.

"I got that, Paige," Jake said shortly, staring at the ground. His hand clenched in a fist.

I cringed at his harshness, but I needed to finish. "I also wanted to tell you not to worry about Saturday. I'm sure things are busy, so . . ." I trailed off.

"Saturday?" Jake repeated. "Right. The wedding." He spread his fingers across his forehead and with his thumb and middle finger massaged his temples. "Paige," he said, and for a brief moment I thought he was going to assure me he would be there.

I was reminded of the time I thought I had baked a cake to perfection. I'd carefully removed it from the oven and set it down with a smile. Slowly, the middle of the cake began a downward descent. My smile had caved with the cake, which ended up boasting a giant sinkhole and tasting like a bitter flour-filled chocolate bar.

"Look, I'm sorry. I just . . ." Jake's words drifted off with his gaze, and I turned around to see Lucy walking toward us. Jake's eyes snapped from her to me. "I can't do this right now."

My mouth pressed my cheeks upward, but we both knew my smile was not sincere. I swallowed my initial words and waited for my head to clear before responding. "Sure," I mumbled, feeling myself fall deeper into the sinkhole he'd created. "I totally understand," I lied and scrunched my face together. I probably looked like a pouting duck. "I'll pray for you." I took a step backward.

"Don't bother," he said. "Prayers don't work." He turned and walked away.

I didn't watch him go. I couldn't. My mind was swimming around and around in a muddle of anger, confusion, and hurt. Humiliation and self-doubt were mixed in too, but in that moment, I only wanted to scream, to run, to do something to make the thought of Jake leave my mind and my heart.

Mom appeared at my side. She put her arm around my shoulders. "Let's go to Millie's for lunch," she suggested.

Conversation was nil during the ride and most of our meal. Mom valiantly avoided all things Jake-related and talked instead about Max's latest feat (opening the fridge), Dad's vexation with a dry patch of lawn, and Matt's new declared major—travel and tourism.

I finished off my chocolate caramel custard and drove Mom home. "Thanks," I said as I pulled into the driveway.

"For?" Mom raised her eyebrows.

I rolled my eyes and then scooped her hand into mine. "For coming to the funeral, for picking up the tab at lunch, and for not asking," I said.

"Hmm," Mom mused. I was certain she wanted to say more and grateful when she didn't. "Okay, then." She gathered her purse from the floor and opened her door.

"Mom?" I asked.

She looked at me.

"Can I borrow Dad on Saturday night?" I hated the surrender in my voice.

"Oh, honey." Mom leaned over and gave me a hug, and even though the corner of the console pressed painfully into my side, it was nice. "I'll make sure he's dressed properly, and then he's all yours."

I didn't know one day could cover such a spectrum of emotion. I'd bounced from excitement to sorrow to fear to anger and somehow ended up on gratitude. Had my mother always been so great? And more importantly, why had I failed to notice?

CHAPTER 22
I Waltzed

THANKFULLY, BETWEEN WORK AND WEDDING preparations, the remainder of the week passed quickly. Mandy had paid for a professional manicure for herself earlier in the week, but on Thursday night we played salon. She painted my fingernails, and we gave each other pedicures. She wanted to spend her last night with her family, so I spent Friday evening alone, writing lesson plans and watching a poor modern-day remake of Jane Austen's *Emma*. Saturday dawned beautiful and lonely.

I woke with the sun but didn't need to arrive for pictures until three. The ceremony was scheduled for five, followed by dinner and the reception. I tossed in bed for forty minutes before admitting I wasn't going to get any more sleep and deciding to head outside for a run.

I pushed myself hard, rhythmically counting my footfalls to keep my mind from straying to unwanted topics. After the funeral I had focused on Mandy, but in the quiet hours each night, my thoughts had wandered to Jake. I wondered what he was doing. Was Lucy able to pull him from his funk? His mother would have known what to do. Did his father? Had Jake allowed God into his life to help him heal? Had his smile returned? Did he ever think of me?

I'd only received messages from Mom, Heather, and Mandy, plus one random message from someone at the district office wanting to know if I would share my military contact so they could invite them to the high-school job fair. I looked up the number for the local recruiter and forwarded his name instead of Jake's.

I would welcome a call from Jake. In fact, I desperately wanted one, and because of my desperation, I knew I was in trouble. However, it also gave me the strength to be patient. With Gavin I'd let myself become abused. I refused to let the same thing happen with Jake. I refused to chase him. If he wanted to see me again, the next step was his to make.

Heather showed up at noon with takeout. We chatted about the kids and ate, then made a list of all the trips we wanted Matt to get us discounts on if he actually graduated in travel and tourism before switching his major again.

Mandy planned on wearing her hair down and had asked for her attendants to pull their hair back into some sort of ponytail or braid. Heather served as my go-to girl for all special occasions, and the internet amped up her game. She spread eight different pictures of hairdo possibilities across the table.

"Voilá!" she said and waved her hands over the options with a flourish. "Now you need to pick one."

I eyed them all. "That's going to be hard. These are all great."

Heather sat back and crossed her arms. "You'll have to be in more weddings, and then we can try them all. Better yet, get married yourself and have lots of pre-wedding parties."

"Yeah right." I scoffed.

I'd been a mess the last few days, and I really wanted to feel beautiful. I hoped wearing a pretty dress, sparkly shoes, and donning model-worthy makeup would somehow lift my spirits. Sure, my dad was my date, but there were bound to be other single men in attendance. If I caught someone looking twice my way, I'd at least have hope that one day Mr. Right might introduce himself. The problem was that the only person I wanted to look beautiful for wouldn't be attending.

I chose a loose diagonal braid, and Heather secured the twist below my ear. She curled thick wavy ringlets in the long ends and arranged them to flow over my left shoulder. Heather didn't ask for my input on my makeup, and I let her have free reign. She lined my eyes in black, then blended neutral-colored sparkly eye shadows to make my eyes pop. With a light powder foundation, mascara, and lip liner and color, Heather had worked her fairy-godmother magic. She helped me into the coral dress, and I slipped on the sparkly silver heels. I felt like a princess. I twirled twice in the mirror for good measure, then gave my sister a huge hug.

"Thanks," I said.

"Jake's missing out," she said with sympathy.

I nodded my head once. "Yes, he is."

Heather handed me my silver clutch and a cream-colored wrap. "Go have fun tonight. You deserve it."

There was no need for Dad to come two hours early, so I drove to Dunlap Gardens alone. Mom would drop Dad by later, and I planned to head back to their house and stay the night.

I squealed when I saw Mandy. She looked amazing. Her entire wedding had been about simplicity, and looking at her dress, I envied the concept. The top of her dress matched the wrap style of the bridesmaids' dresses, and where the bodice met her waistline, it disappeared into a wide satin ribbon that encircled her waist. The ends of the ribbon were tied into a perfect bow on her left hip, then trailed gracefully to the floor. Mandy wore another piece of wide ribbon as a headband, and the contrast of the white against her dark hair was stunning.

"Has Brandon seen you yet?" I asked.

Her face glowed with joy. "No," she said. "That's bad karma."

"You look beautiful!" I held her hands and leaned in to hug her carefully.

"So do you," she said, spreading our arms wide. "Man! We clean up good."

I giggled and followed Mandy to where her mom stood talking with one of the employees. Mandy hadn't taken bridal pictures prior to her wedding day because she said she wanted her pictures to capture her joy of the actual event. Taking pictures weeks earlier seemed absurd to her. There was something to her reasoning because as I followed her around, arranging her dress, and holding flowers while the photographer clicked away, Mandy glowed. Her smile shined sincere, and her joy was evident in every shot. The natural color warming her cheeks remained throughout the entire ninety-minute shoot.

I watched her with envy. But her joy was so real I couldn't help the smile that spread across my face. How could I not be happy for her?

Brandon and the rest of the bridal party arrived about thirty minutes prior to the ceremony. Mandy, her mother, and I moved to the bride's waiting room, where Mandy greeted her three bridesmaids and applied a fresh coat of lipstick. They all gushed over her dress and hair, and I stood in the corner watching happily.

After a faint knock on the door, my dad popped his head around the corner. He looked a little embarrassed as all the ladies turned to look at him, but he finally spotted me.

"Hey, honey," he said. "Just wanted you to know I'm here."

I walked over to the door and gave him a kiss on the cheek. "Thanks, Dad. I'll see you afterward, okay?" I said as I wiped the lipstick off his face. I took comfort in knowing I had one man in my life I could always count on.

Dad left to find a seat, and the bridesmaids shared a final round of hugs before the director told us it was time to line up. Mandy had also simplified by refusing to have a wedding rehearsal. She claimed we'd all watched enough television to know how things should work. She instructed us to walk nice and slow and smile. Simple enough.

We lined up with the groomsmen, who wore gray three-piece suits and matching coral-colored ties. Brandon's brother escorted the first bridesmaid down the garden path, followed by Mandy's brother and Brandon's sister. The best man was a friend of Brandon's named Oliver. We'd met several months ago when Mandy and I had delivered food to all the guys who helped Brandon pack up for his move to Southern California.

Oliver stepped beside me and offered his arm. He leaned toward my ear and whispered above the music, "Hello again, Paige. You look lovely."

"Thank you," I said and slipped my arm through his. "You look rather resplendent yourself."

Oliver laughed quietly at my word choice, and we began our promenade toward the ivy-covered trellis.

Oliver did look nice with his black hair and light-brown skin. His eyes were contemplative and happy. I'd noticed him when we had first met, but since I'd been dating Gavin at the time, I hadn't thought anymore about him.

Walking down the aisle of grass, I spotted my dad. He winked at me as I passed, and I felt a lift in my heart, considering two men had acknowledged me. My thoughts reluctantly returned to Jake, and I didn't understand how I could miss him at the same time I wanted to flaunt the fact that I was good enough and pretty enough for someone else to take notice of me. Regardless of how I wanted Jake to feel, none of it mattered, because he wasn't here.

When we reached the minister, I gave Oliver a flirty smile before stepping aside to my position. He granted me a mischievous grin and released my arm.

Take that, Jake Summers.

While Mandy dismissed some traditions, she held tightly to others. The minister offered some counsel and performed the ceremony, and then Mandy and Brandon exchanged vows and rings, which was followed by the final pronouncement that they were officially husband and wife. The happy couple fairly floated down the aisle. Oliver and I followed with a little more decorum. We turned a corner and walked out of sight of the guests, only to find Mandy and Brandon kissing much more intimately than they had in front of the minister.

Oliver laughed. "Now, that's how it's done."

Mandy's cheeks grew bright red as she pulled away from Brandon.

"Oh no, you don't." Brandon tugged her back to him for one more kiss.

I whistled a catcall, and Oliver winked at me.

The photographer posed the happy couple for more pictures, after which we followed them to a receiving line inside the formal gardens. Once Dad had congratulated Mandy, I excused myself to sit with him for a bit.

While Dad went through the buffet line, I got a glass of punch for him and grabbed myself a water.

"Thanks again for coming, Dad," I said after we found a table. "I haven't been able to see you, so I guess you could have stayed home." I took a drink. "Although, you look rather dashing all dressed up."

"I just do what your mom tells me to do." Dad smiled and pretended to straighten his tie. "Besides, I like seeing you like this." Dad flicked his chin toward me.

"Dressed up?" I asked.

"Well, you do look beautiful and way too grown-up." Dad leaned close and covered the side of his mouth with his hand to share his secret. "I understand why all the guys keep staring at you."

"Yeah right," I said with a laugh.

"It's true," Dad said. "I saw the way the best man was checking you out. I'm watching him." I laughed again, and Dad continued. "But what I meant was I like seeing you happy. Your smile has been gone the last few days, and I've missed it."

"I can't help it today. I mean, look at Mandy—she's glowing; she's so happy. Some of her joy must have rubbed off." I watched Brandon whisper something in Mandy's ear. She nodded, and a minute later they began walking the length of the receiving line to greet the last few guests.

Dad watched with me. "They both look very happy. Today their lives have changed for the better."

We watched Mandy and Brandon walk to the head table. "I'd better go get Mandy some food." I stood up and touched my dad's shoulder. "I'll be back in a while."

"Take your time. Go do your duty," Dad said and waved me away. "Just save me a dance."

"Deal," I agreed and bent over to kiss his cheek again before walking to the buffet.

Oliver stood in the food line and motioned for me to join him. "The bridal party is allowed to cut," he said softly near my ear.

"Good, 'cause I'm starving," I said and stepped directly in front of him.

We talked casually about Oliver's job as a software developer and then delivered plates to the bride and groom before returning to the line to scrounge for ourselves. Oliver asked about my work at the school and told me his sister's experience in speech class. His exaggerated tales were hilarious, and I laughed all the way through dinner.

Mandy hadn't hired a deejay. Instead she and Brandon had created a playlist of their favorite songs and let them play through. They finished their food, Brandon led Mandy out for the first dance, and afterward they motioned for the wedding party to join them.

Oliver held out his hand. "Shall we?"

"We shall," I replied and let him lead me to the floor.

The song was not especially slow, but Oliver followed Brandon's lead, and rather than dance individually, he placed one hand at my waist and with the other held on to my hand, guiding me around the floor in a fast-paced version of a waltz. Oliver's feet moved quickly, and I laughed as I stumbled to keep up with him.

"Sorry." I giggled when I misstepped again. "I'm throwing off your mojo."

My body moved forward instead of back, and Oliver tightened his grip to keep us both from tumbling. I looked up, saw his grin, and laughed again.

"You're enjoying tormenting me. You could slow down, you know, before I knock us both onto our backsides," I said.

"Nah," Oliver said as he twirled me out under his arm and pulled me back again. "I like hearing your laugh."

"Why, Oliver," I said in a teasing tone, "I do believe you're flirting with me."

"Pretty and perceptive," he said.

The song ended, and as the next began, the dance floor filled with people. Oliver and I danced near each other for two more songs, laughing as we demonstrated our best dorky dance moves.

When the next slow song began, Oliver held out his hand. I took a step toward him, then heard my dad's voice. "Would it be all right if I claimed Paige for this one?" Oliver and I turned to see him standing there. "I am, after all, her date."

"Dad, meet Oliver. Oliver, my dad, Nathan Hall." I watched while the men shook hands.

"Do you have a date you need to ask to dance?" Dad asked Oliver, and I swatted his arm.

Oliver laughed. "No, sir. I'm here on my own tonight."

"Well, thanks for letting me cut in," Dad said. He took my hand, and Oliver walked away. "He seems like a nice enough guy."

"Yeah, he does," I agreed.

"Nice enough to make you forget about Jake?" Dad asked.

"Ahh, Dad. You really need to read a Jane Austen novel," I said.

"Why? Do her heroines forget about guys who have wronged them when they dance with other guys who make them laugh?" Dad asked.

"No. And Jake didn't wrong me," I said defensively.

"No?" Dad asked.

"No. He just . . . I don't know; he's dealing with a lot. I guess he needs to figure some things out." My heart throbbed with my words. Dad had asked the question I didn't have the answer to. "Believe me, I haven't forgotten him," I said quietly.

Sadly, it was the truth. Oliver was a happy diversion. Conversation came easily, and we were both dressed up and ready to play make-believe for the night, but my heart didn't respond to Oliver the way it did to Jake. If Jake asked for more time, I could give him time. If he wanted to move forward, even better. The problem was that he hadn't asked for anything. He'd left me cold and alone and broken and wondering which direction to turn. Did we have a future? Did he miss me? Would he call?

The questions circled in time with the dance. Dad used to let us stand on his toes when we were little. He would turn a circle, and then Heather and I would switch out for the next round. At the very end he would spin us until we were dizzy, and we would stagger forward until we fell over laughing.

I no longer stood on Dad's toes, but as we rotated around again and again, thoughts of Jake crowded my head. I felt dizzy and off-balance. And of course, I wasn't laughing.

Dad attempted a fast song, claiming it was the proper thing a date would do. But his dance moves endangered the other guests, so I suggested we take a break. He didn't argue.

Mandy and Brandon cut the cake, each feeding the other a piece, properly and politely. The perfection kind of made me want to gag, but I clapped with the other guests and delivered a piece of cake to my dad.

Mandy nixed the whole toss-the-bouquet tradition, which totally suited me. And when the newlyweds returned to the dance floor, Oliver came and asked if I would dance with him again. Dad waved me off, and after one song, Oliver noticed my spunk had vanished.

"Are you sure you want to dance?" he asked. "Or is there somewhere else you'd rather be?"

I looked around at the beautiful setting. "I heard the gardens are beautiful. Should we go explore?"

"Sure." Oliver stepped aside and lightly touched my back as I walked by.

Various paths twisted around in a maze. Low hedges, flowering trees, artistically placed lights, benches, and fountains. Jane Austen would be proud.

"So who is he?" Oliver asked with a sideways smirk.

My eyes grew wide. I shivered from a cool breeze, and Oliver immediately shrugged out of his jacket and draped it over my shoulders.

"Thanks," I said.

"Come on. Out with it," he said. "I'm a good listener."

"Very well. You asked for it," I said, and then I told him all of it. Oliver learned about Gavin and my near-death experience in the parking lot with Jake. I explained about wanting to take things slow and how I'd thought things were going great with Jake. Our late-night talks in the hospital, meeting each other's families, and bonding with Jake's mom were all signs of forward progression. Until everything had come to a screeching halt.

Oliver listened patiently, walking beside me with his hands in his pockets and nodding or commenting at all the right times. It felt good to say everything aloud. Oliver was a good sounding board, and although I barely knew him, I didn't feel judged.

After I finished dishing, Oliver stopped walking. He stepped in front of me and turned to face me. "He'll come around," he said.

I pulled the jacket tighter and looked down at my shiny silver shoes. "I don't know. Two weeks ago I didn't have any doubts." I stood up straight. "Now doubts are all I have."

"No, I'm telling you. This Jake guy won't let you simply walk away," Oliver assured me.

"How do you know?" I asked.

"Because, from what you told me, you make him happy. That's worth fighting for . . . isn't that right, Jake?"

The easy mood instantly dropped away. I turned around and saw Jake standing on the path, and the moment felt like something out of a novel. He wore a black fitted suit with a plain black tie, and he looked amazing. I blinked several times to make sure Jake wasn't a hallucination. My heart froze, and I couldn't have spoken even if I had wanted to. I looked back at Oliver, who shrugged and gave me a small crooked smile.

"Hi," Jake said. Gone was the pilot ego I often teased him about. He took a single step toward me, then stopped. His eyes never left mine, and he asked, "Are we still doing the whole honesty thing?"

I swallowed my shock and answered, "Of course." Oliver moved to stand beside me.

"Is this your date?" Jake asked.

I turned to look at Oliver; his eyes darted to mine, and I knew if I'd wanted to lie or make Jake jealous, Oliver would play along. But I kept my promise to Jake.

"No. When you . . . had a change of plans, my dad stepped in as my date. This is Oliver, Brandon's best man," I said. Jake probably wanted more of an explanation, but I'd answered his question and didn't feel inclined to expound.

Oliver lifted his hand from his pocket, and with two fingers saluted Jake. I couldn't help smiling a little. I hadn't told Oliver about Jake's military background, and I found the salute very ironic.

Jake didn't flinch or smile or anything. Instead he stepped forward and extended his hand. "Hi, Oliver. Jake Summers." He looked back at me. "May I talk to you for a minute?"

Jake's coming had to be a good sign. He'd been in stealth mode long enough that if he'd wanted to never see me again, he could have walked away, free and clear. And while my head told me I should talk with him, my heart tumbled with uncertainty. It didn't want to feel pain again. I had grown accustomed to the numbness that had seeped in over the last two weeks. Feeling was hard.

Oliver turned to face me and blocked my view of Jake. "I'll stay if you want me to," he said.

"I think I should talk to him," I said.

Oliver smiled wide. "So do I. I think he makes you happy, too."

I pulled his jacket from my shoulders and handed it back to him. "Thanks, Oliver."

He stepped back and slid his arms into his suit coat. "Well, I need to make sure a certain car was decorated properly." He tipped his head to the side. "Thanks for the dance, Paige."

I watched Oliver walk down the twinkle-light path before I looked back at Jake.

"Paige." His chest rose and fell. "I'm sorry."

Cold air layered us in a shroud of privacy. Light music floated across the air, muting the voices from the wedding and creating a surreal ambiance. I stood frozen, as if in the climax of an Austen romance, and wondered if my story would have a happy ending. I crossed my arms over my chest and watched Jake.

"I've missed you," he said. He shoved his hands into his pockets and looked at the ground. "I know I screwed up and you don't need to hear my lame excuses." He exhaled loudly and shook his head. "If Mom were here, she'd kill me."

I narrowed my eyes and wondered what he meant. "Is that why you're here?" I asked. "Because you think she'd want you to come?"

While I was glad to see him, his motivation needed to stem from what he wanted. He needed to take time for me because I was important to him, not to please his deceased mother.

"Yes. And no," he said.

I tensed with a sudden shiver. Jake extended his arms. "May I?" he asked. "I promise I'll explain everything, but I can't do it if you're too numb to hear me." He smiled meekly.

As much as I wanted to run into his embrace, I couldn't. Not before we talked. "I don't know if now's a good time. I need to get back to Mandy." I rubbed my hands up and down my arms to chase the chill away.

Jake's arms fell back to his side. "I don't want to leave," he said quickly. "I mean, I'll wait while you do what you need to do. Then can we talk?"

"That's all I've wanted from you." I could barely speak without tears forming in my eyes. I blinked rapidly.

"Can I walk you back?" Jake held out his hand. "Then I'll stay out of the way until you're ready."

The invitation of Jake's open palm was more than I could resist. I slid my hand into his.

"You look incredible," Jake whispered.

We reached the party, and Jake squeezed my hand, but my mind was too jumbled to return the gesture. "I'll be waiting," he said before I walked away.

Mandy said goodbye to her parents, and I saw my cue to distribute sparklers to the guests. Fireworks seemed an appropriate way to send a couple off on their honeymoon.

The other bridesmaids helped me pass out the long metal wands, and when Brandon gave the okay, the groomsmen lit the sparklers. Mandy and Brandon held hands and walked together through the crackling rain. Oliver had decorated the car tastefully, and Brandon kissed Mandy before opening her door. Mandy emanated happiness as she climbed into the car, and my heart lightened. For the first time that night, I felt hopeful.

CHAPTER 23
I Listened

I HELPED THE OTHER ATTENDANTS gather the used sparklers, and we stuck them into a bucket of sand. Several guests followed the exit of the bride and groom, while others mingled or wandered back to the dance floor. As I circled the lawn, I saw Jake sitting at a table with my father and wished I could swoop around like a hummingbird and listen to their conversation.

I needed a few more minutes to settle my nerves before speaking with Jake. I returned to the bride's room and grabbed my wrap and purse. When I walked up to the table, both men stood.

No one spoke. They both stared at me as I looked back and forth between them. I pulled my wrap tighter.

Finally, Dad broke the tension. "Is there anything else you need to do?"

I shook my head. "No. At least, not for the wedding." A sudden cold trickled into my chest.

Dad turned toward Jake and stared at him. Jake shifted and then asked, "Do you want to talk tonight, or would another time be better?"

I watched Jake's face, trying to get a read on him, but his emotions were hidden behind his eyes. "Do *you* want to wait for another time?" I asked. As much as I wanted to hear what he had to say, I refused to force his hand.

"No," he answered quickly. His abruptness made Dad's eyebrows shoot up. "I mean, I'd like to explain myself. But you've been patient with me, and I'm sure you've had a long day. I'll let you decide."

I took a long drawn-out breath. It had been an exhausting day, both emotionally and physically, but I knew if I went home without hearing Jake out, I wouldn't sleep. It was time to hear his explanation. It was time to listen.

"Can you take me home?" I asked Jake.

"Of course," he said, and his face lightened when he realized that meant we could talk.

I pulled my car keys from my purse and handed them to my dad. "I shouldn't have made you come. I'm sorry you had a lousy night."

"It wasn't lousy," Dad said.

"You're a bad liar," I said. I wrapped one arm around Dad's back and rested my head on his shoulder.

"I could claim the most beautiful girl as my daughter. How does that classify as lousy?" Dad hugged me back. Then he whispered into my ear, "Your smile returned tonight. Don't let yourself lose it again."

"Okay," I said and let him go. "But it's kind of out of my hands."

Dad turned to Jake. "Bring her home safe—and happy," he said firmly.

Jake automatically straightened and replied, "I'll do my best, sir."

I thought he might even salute, but he didn't. Instead he and Dad stared at each other for an extra-long minute until Dad seemed satisfied. Then Dad kissed my cheek and walked away.

I wanted the memories of Mandy's wedding to remain joyful and free of whatever happened with Jake. Going back to my empty house felt too intimate, and neither of us wanted to sit and talk in the car. We settled on Millie's and asked for a corner booth. I ordered my favorite hot chocolate, and Jake asked for a glass of water.

After sitting in silence for five minutes, I said, "Millie's closes in an hour. I'm not sure what you want to say, but maybe we should start talking."

Jake pressed his lips together and moved his hands from the table to his lap and then back to the table. The waitress brought our drinks, and when she walked away, Jake began, "First of all, I owe you an apology."

I wrapped my hands around my cocoa but kept my eyes fixed on Jake.

"It was wrong of me to bail on you tonight, and by the time Lucy knocked some sense into me, I had to run back to my house to grab my suit. I didn't think I should appear in my uniform," he said with a shrug.

"So you're apologizing for tonight?" I asked.

He had to realize there was more. He couldn't simply shrug away the fact that he hadn't called or texted or acknowledged my existence for the last twelve days. Nor could he dismiss his callousness at the funeral. Mourning was to be expected. Pain and grief, yes. But Jake had been downright rude.

"Yes . . . and for the past few weeks," Jake said, and I began to hope he was ready to balance the scales. "My mom really liked you, Paige. And truthfully, you remind me of her. That was part of the problem."

I startled and leaned back. I didn't know where this was headed, but I did know whatever had happened between us was not my fault. If Jake placed the onus on me, the conversation was over.

He grabbed my hand before I could pull away. "That was *my* problem," he said, and my frustration tapered. I let my hand sit limply in his, not knowing which way to fall. "My mom was the most positive person I knew. She looked at everything with bright, happy eyes. She saw the best in everyone; she expected the best from everyone. She was always hopeful, and she never questioned God." Jake pressed the pads of his fingertips into the palm of my hand. "You're the same way. You don't judge. Your smile lifts everyone around you. You emanate light and goodness, and your faith doesn't waver."

"You make me sound—"

"Like an angel? A goddess?" Jake cut in. His lips pushed into enough of a smile that his dimple appeared.

"Now I'm calling your bluff," I said, but I let my fingers relax around his.

"I'm serious, Paige," Jake said. Then he got quiet.

He stared at our hands, and his thumb began to stroke my skin. Tiny embers ignited somewhere deep inside me, tiny flickers of colorful hope like the sparklers from the wedding. They snapped and crackled, and the strings binding my heart began to unravel.

Jake looked back up at me. "I had a lot of anger about my mom. She was so good, and it didn't seem fair. Why would God take her? Why did He let her suffer? When you came to visit in the hospital, everything seemed better. And I was torn. How could I be happy when next to me my mom was in so much pain?" His voice caught, and his fingers stilled in mine. I squeezed his hand, and with tears in his eyes he continued. "I felt like I needed to mourn with her, to suffer with her, and being with you felt like an escape, an easy way out. When I was with you, I felt better, and I felt like I was betraying my mom." A tear rolled down Jake's cheek, and he swiped it away.

"After she died, I knew if I called, you would remind me that God was aware of me and that Mom was now with Him. Your words would comfort me. You would know exactly what to say, and even if you said nothing, holding you would bring me peace, and honestly, I didn't want to feel peace. I wanted to be angry. Angry at the doctors, angry at the disease, angry at God. If my mom couldn't have peace, why should I?" Another tear fell. Jake released my hand and blew his nose into his napkin.

I scooted off my bench and took a step to stand in front of Jake. He raised his blue eyes to mine, and I motioned for him to move over. I slid in next to him and leaned against his shoulder. He sat still and sniffled a few more times. Then he shifted and wrapped his arm around me.

"This is exactly why I didn't call. I wasn't ready for this." His arm tightened. "You know exactly what I need, just like my mom did." He let out a short laugh. "And I guess Lucy too. They both told me not to mess up with you." He squeezed me again.

I lifted my head, leaned back, and took his hand in mine. "Are you ready now?" I looked at our hands, then back up at him.

"I can't promise there won't be rough days." Jake squeezed my fingers. "You know my faith isn't as strong as yours, but I'm working on it. I'm trying to trust God."

I squeezed his fingers back. "Is it working? Trusting God?"

"It's hard to turn it over to Him. But I've been praying for strength and understanding." Jake slowly nodded. "My soul still aches, but I also feel lighter."

"Your mom would be proud," I said. "I believe she does have peace now. She would want you to be happy."

"You make me happy." Jake raised his eyes to mine, and the moment pulled taut. Our breath collided in electric shocks between us. Our connection was undeniable, and I wondered if Jake would verbalize the emotion, the feelings burning deeper with every heartbeat. He tugged me forward. His head bent down, and he pressed his forehead to mine.

Jake was saying all the right words, but my tender heart needed affirmation. "I'm glad Lucy convinced you to come, but I can't do this if you're going to disappear again." I took a shuddering breath and pulled back. "You really hurt me."

Jake reached his free hand forward and cupped my face. "I was selfish, and I'm so sorry. I promise I'm not going anywhere." He leaned forward, and I closed my eyes as he placed a kiss on my forehead.

I leaned back in to his shoulder, and we sat quietly and contently until the waitress told us they were closing. Jake paid the bill, then grabbed my hand. "Come on; I have an idea," he said.

He wouldn't give me any hints as he drove, and by the time we pulled into my driveway, my nerves were on overdrive. "I don't think we should go inside," I said. His touch was intoxicating, and I knew my limits.

"We're not," Jake said.

I watched quizzically while he fumbled with his radio and then his phone. He rolled down the windows, then walked around and opened my door. "I still need to dance with the most beautiful girl at the wedding. Would you do me the honor, Miss Hall?" Jake asked, bowing low.

I stepped from the car and spread my skirt wide as I curtsied. "It would be my pleasure."

In one smooth movement, Jake had me wrapped in his arms. A guitar strummed the melody, slow and steady, and our bodies swayed in a small circle. Jake twirled me outward and then spun me in and dipped me low. I giggled as he lifted me upright.

The music continued, but our movement froze. Jake pulled me close and held on tight. I rested my head on his chest, and he whispered into my hair, "Can you forgive me, Paige? For not calling? For being a brute at the funeral? For ditching the wedding? I've missed you."

I mumbled my contentment, and when he pulled back and looked at me, I gave him an audible yes. After another breath I told him the truth. "I've missed you too."

Then Jake kissed me with passion and fierceness. His lips explored mine before moving to my cheek and temple. My hands tangled in his hair as he made his way back to my mouth. His arms wrapped around my waist, pulling me closer to him, and his kisses grew soft, leaving me no doubt about the sincerity of his apology. Breathless, I broke away, now thankful for the cool night air.

I looked at him. Determination filled his eyes, confirming his resolve to make things right. "I'm glad you came tonight," I said, knowing my cheeks burned red. I smiled. "And I think it's good we stayed outside."

"Me too," Jake said, and then he kissed me again. The tenderness in this kiss spoke volumes. He cherished me, and I knew it. I closed my eyes and allowed myself to forget everything else so I could embrace this moment. Jake cradled me in his arms, and I focused on the security, the rightness of it all, the feeling of his hands moving to my hair, the warmth of his nearness.

This wasn't a moment filled with passion. This kiss represented the promise of a future. A promise that I wasn't the only one falling in love.

CHAPTER 24
I Stargazed

I SLEPT SOUNDLY FOR THE first time in weeks. Dad called Sunday morning asking random questions about the weather and my health. I knew he was checking up on me, like a good father should. When he began asking if I wanted him to come set gopher traps in the yard, I stopped him midquestion and told him about my conversation with Jake. I couldn't read my dad's reaction over the phone, but I think in the end he decided if I could forgive Jake, he could too. He also asked if he could update my mother before church, and without hesitation I agreed.

To know Jake had turned to God, that he was trying to trust Him, warmed my soul. To know he considered me a source of comfort and joy was oddly flattering. I couldn't see him Sunday because he had to drive home and get ready to head back to work. Colonel Halton had promised Jake he could forgo any long trips for the next couple of weeks while he helped his dad finalize things, but Jake still had a lot to catch up on.

He called me over Bluetooth; we chatted for the hour he drove home, and I hung up happy. Dad had spread the word about Jake's apology, so by the time I arrived for Sunday dinner, the conversation had migrated to other topics.

Monday and Tuesday progressed as normal, but I missed Mandy. I didn't want to bother her, but I did send one text with a brief explanation of what had happened with Jake. She replied with an emoji of a kissy face, and I wondered which one of us she referenced.

Wednesday, at lunch, I found Jake had left a voicemail. *"Sorry to bother you during work. I'm coming down to stay with my dad for the night. Can I take you to dinner around eighteen thirty?"*

I texted him back. *I got your message. I don't want to take time from your dad.*
Jake: *I'm staying the night, and I'm taking Dad to breakfast.*

Me: *Are you sure?*

Jake: *Yes. Please say you can come.*

Me: *I can come.*

Jake: *Dress casual.*

He showed up at my door in jeans, flip-flops, and a button-down black shirt. He looked good. He always looked good. I left on the blue chevron-striped maxiskirt and cardigan I'd worn to work, but I swapped my wedges for tan sandals.

Jake greeted me with a sweet kiss on the cheek, and after we got into his car and pulled out of the driveway, he insisted we eat at Casa de Taco.

"It's my apology go-to restaurant," he said, and I noticed his smirk.

"What are you apologizing for?" I asked.

"Nothing new. I'm still trying to make up for . . . before." He grimaced.

At the restaurant, we were seated at an odd corner table. Jake didn't care for the arrangement, so he pulled his chair around, and we sat at a forty-five-degree angle, with only the corner of the table separating us. We ate and talked about work until the subject turned to Jake's dad.

"How's he doing?" I asked.

"Lucy's been great," Jake said. "She stays at the house with him so he won't be all alone. He's been married to Mom for thirty-seven years. He misses her. He's not ready to go through her things, and I don't know if he will be for a while." Jake ran his hand through his hair. "Lucy and I have talked about having him go visit his brother for a few weeks so we can clean out Mom's stuff, but I don't know how he'd react to the idea. Right now he's taking it a day at a time."

I watched Jake and felt more irrational flattery. My face must have revealed my strange pleasure.

Jake stopped talking and looked at me sideways. "What?"

"I'm sorry. I guess I feel honored you would share this with me." I felt silly for saying it out loud, and I could feel the color rise in my cheeks, but I'd promised honesty. "It makes things feel balanced."

"You mean I'm actually being a decent boyfriend?" Jake asked.

"Is that what you are?" I asked. My cheeks grew warmer. "My boyfriend?" The word sounded nice.

"Most definitely. No one else is allowed to make you blush like that," Jake said. His large smile and dimple appeared. "And no one else is allowed to do this either."

He grabbed the leg of my chair and pulled me closer to him. He leaned over and kissed me. Not a quick peck on the lips but a long, delicious, make-my-heart-speed kiss.

After Jake pulled away, I sighed dramatically. "Okay. You can be my boyfriend."

"Thanks, girlfriend," Jake said, and although his tone was teasing, I knew he was completely serious, and I was completely okay with it.

Days and weeks passed, and Jake returned to his regular flying schedule. Regular wasn't a great definition for it because his trips were sporadic and often crept up with very little warning. I got good practice at being flexible, and Jake tried hard to keep me informed. The whole scale analogy helped me keep perspective. We talked every night, and Jake promised that the only positive of being on the road was when he got to watch the Kings' hockey games in his hotel room without feeling guilty. I razzed him a little for his hockey binge, but we agreed hockey to him was like Austen to me. We would watch it for one another, but we didn't actually enjoy it.

During the time Jake was gone, I volunteered to help my mom with her projects. Patty's passing helped me realize how precious time could be. Mom and I had hit a reset button on our relationship, and things were going well. We both worked hard to acknowledge what was important to each other.

Mom learned to be patient too. It took an extra week to sew new curtains because Jake returned from a longer trip and was given some bonus leave. I told Mom I'd stick around and help her finish, but she waved me away and said the curtains could wait.

Jake had become Matt's number-one competition on the Xbox. One Friday night we stopped by my parents and found Matt there too. Jake and Matt got into a vicious digital basketball showdown.

"Woo-hoo!" Matt called after his player dunked an alley-oop.

Jake shook his head and chuckled. "We need to invest in a hockey video game."

"Wouldn't matter." Matt clicked a combination of buttons on his game controller. "Goals, buckets, touchdowns . . . I'm in the zone."

"Cocky much?" I asked.

Matt's virtual player tossed a long shot at the buzzer. "Sweetness!" Matt called as the ball swished through the net.

Jake tossed his controller onto the cushion beside him. "I give up."

Our happy routine continued. Work, phone calls with Jake, dates with Jake, spending time with both of our families, and his trips—or TDYs, as Jake called them—filled our schedules. Every time Jake smiled at me or took my hand, I wondered how I'd been fortunate enough to get to call this man mine.

Roughly eight weeks after Mandy's wedding, Miranda walked into my classroom with another armful of lilies. "These were brought in for you, Miss Hall," she said, smiling as she put them on my desk. "I asked the delivery man for a name, and he said they were from Summer Sun Flower Shop." That was the name of Lucy's boutique. Miranda looked over the beautiful blooms and flicked a card. "Yeah, there's a card too, exactly like he said."

I offered my thanks, and when Miranda left, my students started whispering. I smiled. Stargazer lilies—Jake still needed to tell me why he had selected them.

I thought about leaving the arrangement at work so I could enjoy it the following day, but my house was lonely, and the reminder of Jake could keep me company.

Finally, five-thirty rolled around, and I figured it would be safe to call Jake. "You're spoiling me," I said when he picked up.

"I have some time to make up for," he said.

"Will you tell me why you chose the stargazer lilies?" I asked.

"I will. Are you free for a late dinner tomorrow night?"

I leaned over the flowers and inhaled the delicious fragrance. "Dinner sounds great. What time?"

We solidified our plans, and Jake told me to dress warm. Then I watched the snail-like clock and began to count down to when I would see Jake again.

The sun hung low in the sky when Jake knocked on the door. I asked him to pick me up at my parents' because I promised Mom I would teach her how to scan photos and save them to a hard drive. We'd just finished our tutorial when Jake arrived.

He eyed the mounds of boxes Mom had made Dad haul in from the garage. "Wow," he said.

"Those are all my grandmother's pictures. She couldn't resist snapping away at any get-together. It makes me grateful for digital photography," I said.

I picked my coat up off the couch and waved goodbye as I followed Jake outside to Lucy's truck.

"Where are we going?" I asked.

He looked back over his shoulder and smiled wide. "Stargazing."

Jake drove toward the lake, and by the time we arrived, the sky had grown dark. He turned down a dirt road, and I held on to the door handle as we bounced through the ruts.

Tall trees lined both sides of the road, blocking out the stars and enclosing us in an ominous black tunnel. "You did say stargazing, right?" I asked.

"Yep," Jake answered nonchalantly.

My hand gripped the door handle tighter, and I stared at the beam of headlights illuminating the road ahead. Jake smiled and sang along with the rock song streaming through the speakers. His happy confidence convinced me to relax my grip—a little.

The road curved sharply right, and then the sky opened up before us over the wide lake. I unbuckled my seat belt and scooted forward to look out the windshield. The moon was noticeably absent as the pitch black of night draped like a misty veil among the stars. There were thousands of them. Millions of them.

The moment Jake parked the truck, I stepped out. The cold air nipped at my ears, but I didn't care. I wrapped my arms around myself and stared upward. Jake stepped behind me, wrapped his arms around me, and pulled me back against his chest.

"What do you think?" he asked.

"It's amazing! How did you find this place?" I asked and shifted my arms to cross over his.

Jake leaned his chin down toward my ear. "My grandpa used to bring us here to fish. It was our secret family spot. Mom would pack a big picnic, and we'd spend entire afternoons here."

We stood staring skyward until Jake took a step back. "Come on," he said. "Let's eat."

He led me to the bed of the truck, where he laid out several blankets and a gourmet feast. Well, sort of gourmet. Jake had ordered takeout from Millie's: chicken salad sandwiches, fruit, chips, brownies, and of course, an extra-large mug of cinnamon caramel hot chocolate. We wrapped ourselves in blankets and ate a slow meal while Jake pointed out various constellations.

When we'd had enough to eat, we packed the extra food into the basket Jake had brought and sipped on our hot chocolates. Jake fumbled with the blankets, arranging them in one corner of the truck bed, and then he invited me to sit in the circle of his arms. With his warm body behind me and a warm cup of cocoa in my hands, I was idealistically content. I may have even purred.

Jake brushed my hair off my neck and nuzzled near my ear. "Cozy?" he asked.

"Very," I answered and leaned back against him.

"Did you figure it out?" Jake asked.

"What?"

"Stargazing? The stargazer lilies," he said as if it were obvious.

"You promised to tell me." I reached up and lightly pinched him in the bicep. "So out with it."

I felt Jake's chest rise and fall as he drew in a deep breath. "One of the reasons I like flying is because I get a chance to be up there." I followed his gaze upward. "Flying above the clouds can be so peaceful and calm. Those days when I have a perfect flight and perfect weather help me keep my life in perspective. I remember what's really important." Jake rested his chin on the top of my head. "Flying at night is the same but on an entirely different level. Somehow, seeing the stars radiate through the darkness, watching the moon reflect the sun . . . it gives me hope." He shifted to the side, and I turned so we sat face-to-face. "The first time we went out—"

"Because you almost killed me?" I asked with a grin.

"Fine. Because I almost killed you." Jake rolled his eyes, leaned forward, and kissed my forehead. "After you showed up for dinner that night, I felt that same hope. Laughing and talking with you was easy and peaceful, and it reminded me of the star-filled sky." Jake raised his hand and traced my cheekbone with his thumb. "That's why I sent stargazer lilies. That's why I wanted to share this place with you—so you could understand how I feel when I'm with you."

I leaned forward, and when I wrapped my arms around Jake, he reciprocated and held on tight. I couldn't pilot an aircraft through the night sky, but in that moment, I soared among the stars.

CHAPTER 25
I Loved

LIFE CONTINUED MOVING IN A happy dream. I saw Jake less frequently than anyone else I had dated, but in our time together, I grew. In my previous relationships, I had molded to what my boyfriends had needed, what they'd wanted. Things were different with Jake. He brought out the best in me, and I wanted to be the best me because it made me happy. He never tried to change my habits or my ideas. He accepted me wholly and unconditionally. I never fully understood the balance Mandy had described until I lived it. And I realized it wasn't as scary as I had thought.

Mandy had returned from her honeymoon glowing. We ate lunch together almost every day, and one weekend when Brandon had to fly to Chicago, Mandy came over for a sleepover. We binged enough Jane Austen to last for several months.

As we polished off the last of our custard, Mandy yawned and said, "I like Jake."

"Should I be worried? Does Brandon know?" I asked from my seat on the floor and then sucked on my last savory spoonful of yumminess.

"I like him for you." Mandy threw a pillow at me, but it missed.

I pulled the spoon from my mouth and grinned. "Me too."

"Do you see a future with him?" she asked.

I thought about my answer, and a smile appeared before any words left my mouth.

"You do!" Mandy clapped her hands and squealed.

"We haven't talked about anything. I mean, his schedule is super crazy, and I still don't get the whole military thing . . . but I'm trying, and I'm happy."

"Happy like a trip to Disneyland? Or happy like life without Jake is not worth living?"

I laughed and tossed the pillow back at Mandy. "You're so dramatic. Aren't you the one who told me it's all about balance? The thought of being alone doesn't scare me as much as the thought of being without Jake."

"You love him," Mandy said, and her eyes lit.

"I think I do." I didn't attempt to hide my smile.

It wasn't new for me to fall first in a relationship. It seemed I'd always liked my boyfriends more than they'd liked me. I fell faster, and in my past relationships, I had paid for it. Every time.

Ever since my breakup with Gavin, I'd been praying for the strength to know God's path for me. I'd been blessed with peace and counsel from others that helped me better understand my place. The scales in my life were so balanced I didn't feel the need to tell Jake how deeply my emotions ran. I didn't think throwing my heart on the scale would really tilt things one way or the other because everything I did for him was because of those feelings. And I believed the reverse to be true. Jake had shared some intimate thoughts with me. He had promised honesty, and I knew when the time was right, we would talk about a future.

He had made a habit of calling when he got back in town once he finished his debrief and was driving home. But one day he returned from an especially long trip and sent a text that simply read, *I'm home.*

I figured he had texted because he was still on base wrapping things up, and I expected he would call later. But when an hour passed and my phone didn't ring. I wondered if everything was okay.

As my fingers tapped against the screen of my phone, debating whether I should call him, Jake's name lit up the screen. But as I swiped to accept the call, he hung up. I paused with my phone in hand, wondering what had happened. I waited, assuming he would call back, but my screen remained black.

I walked to the kitchen and loaded the dishwasher in an attempt to distract myself. I dried my hands on the dish towel, and when I hung it over the handle of the oven, my phone rang again.

I hesitated for a moment before answering Jake's call. "Hey there. Welcome home," I said.

"Hi," he said flatly. From the background noise, I knew Jake was calling me on Bluetooth.

"How was your trip?" I added extra cheer to my voice.

"Rough." Jake's one-word response left me clambering for what to say next.

"I'm sorry. Anything I can do?" I turned and leaned against the counter.

"Do you know what today is?" Jake asked.

"Um . . . Wednesday, June third? Is that what you mean?" I asked.

"It's been three months since Mom passed," he said and went silent again.

"Three months," I repeated softly. That explained a lot. Months one and two had passed, and Jake kept busy. We often talked about his mom, about happy times and fun stories, and he would become reminiscent but not depressed. This felt different. I took a breath. "Are you okay? Do you want to talk about it or anything?" He had yet to come to me for the hard stuff, and I could feel the raw emotion in his voice, but what else could I offer beyond a listening ear?

I heard Jake sigh. "I know it'll be late by the time I get there, but can I come by?"

My heart lifted. Jake wasn't closing me off; instead he was turning to me.

"I don't especially want to talk; it's just . . . I could use some Paige time today," he said.

"Of course, Jake. I'll be here."

"That's all I need," Jake said.

We hung up, and humble gratitude tugged at my heart. This was balance. This was what a relationship should be. This was right. So right.

Jake came over, and we sat on the couch, where he just held me close. Nothing much was said. He drifted in and out of sleep until just past midnight, when he roused himself enough to drive to his dad's house.

Work the next day was exhausting, but after that night, I knew Jake and I would be okay. We were better together.

On Friday we made plans to go to a cheesy rom-com movie after work. Jake told me he'd pick me up at six, so I was surprised when the final school bell rang and he strode into my classroom.

Seeing his smile, my heart instantly lifted. "Hey," I said. "You're early."

Jake shrugged. "Sorry. I missed you," he said and pulled me into a hug.

"You don't need to be sorry for that." I wrapped my arms around him and snuggled in.

Someone cleared their throat, and I peeked around Jake to see Mandy leaning against the doorframe. "Excuse me, Miss Hall. Aren't you supposed to be working?" She shook her head and tsked. "Hi, Jake," she said.

"Good to see you, Mandy." Jake released his hold but kept one arm around me. "Thanks for hanging out with Paige while I was gone."

"We had a fun weekend. It was nice to catch up and talk about . . . life. Right, Paige?" Mandy asked.

"Right." I turned and smiled at the subject of our *life* talk.

Jake narrowed his eyes and looked between us. "I think I'm missing something, and I think it's probably best if I don't ask. I'm going to sit over here and watch Paige until she's ready to leave." He walked to the corner and folded himself into a small blue chair. He held up his right hand. "I promise I won't interfere with her work, so don't go tattletale to the principal."

"Just no kissing in the classroom, okay?" Mandy said before she turned to leave.

"I make no promises," Jake said under his breath and winked at me.

While I finished lesson plans for the following week, Jake remained quiet, but his mere presence distracted me, plus the fact that Mandy had mentioned kissing, and I couldn't get the thought out of my head.

I worked quickly, and Jake followed me home so we could drop off my car. We grabbed an easy dinner at a pizza joint, then headed to the movie. Jake wanted a brainless flick, and he'd picked the perfect movie. The only redeeming qualities of the movie were the one-liners that were somehow both awful and hilarious.

Back at my house, Jake walked me to the door. "You're not driving all the way home tonight, are you?" I asked.

"No," he said and tucked a piece of my hair behind my ear. "I'm staying at my dad's so I can see you again tomorrow."

"Hmm, sounds good," I said and wrapped my arms around his neck.

He leaned forward and gave me a long and lingering kiss. It was a little slice of heaven, with some crackling thunder woven in. I pulled away with a smile and turned toward the door. As my fingers slipped out of his, he tightened his hold. With his soft tug I turned back around and found Jake staring at me intently. I tilted my head to the side and was about to break the tension by quoting a silly one-liner from the movie, but something in Jake's expression stopped me. The blue in his eyes swirled like a peaceful storm.

"I love you," he said.

A downpour of starry tingles washed over me. My face erupted in a grin I could not restrain.

"Really?" I asked.

Jake laughed lightly, and his dimple appeared. "Yeah. Really."

Warmth pooled inside my stomach, igniting the embers that had lain banked, reserved, and waiting for the moment my emotions could burst into flame. My soul seared with the crackling truth. Jake loved me. I wanted to say it back. I wanted to tell him how I felt and how I'd known I'd loved him for a while. But I was afraid it would sound trite, like I only wanted to mirror his words to balance the scales. So I didn't say anything. I simply squeezed his hand. He squeezed back and looked into my eyes. He had to be able to read my emotions. He had to know how I felt without me audibly saying the words. The tie between us, the connection, was too real to doubt it was anything less than love.

We stood staring at each other, breathing together and grinning like fools while my entire universe fell into balance.

I pushed up on my toes and kissed Jake quickly on the lips. "Good night," I said.

"Sweet dreams, Paige." Jake squeezed my fingers, then let me go.

I stepped through my door and twirled and twirled and twirled until I collapsed on the couch in a happy delirium.

CHAPTER 26
I Waited

JAKE'S CONFESSION SETTLED COMFORTABLY IN my heart. I wanted to tell him how I felt, but not because it was expected. I needed to share those precious words—the *I love you* that encapsulated commitment, emotion, and promise—but I needed a quiet moment when the balance between the two of us felt tangible. In the right moment I could tell him. It hadn't come yet, so I waited.

We continued to see each other as often as our schedules permitted. I was busy my last two weeks of school, filling out reports. A write-up with updates on every student's progress and goals for the following year was required. I also wanted to send each student into summer vacation with several activities and exercises to complete over the break. It all amounted to almost two hours dedicated to each student. I stayed at school until almost six p.m. for two weeks and worked through the weekend.

Jake was a great support. He came down one day and brought takeout, and the next morning he dropped off bagels for Mandy and me before driving back to his house. He sent texts with silly pictures or encouraging words, and on Friday night he personally delivered another bouquet of stargazer lilies.

Family dinner on Sunday was a welcome reprieve. We laughed as Dad updated us on his battle with the gophers, which apparently the gophers were winning. Heather's kids played with Duplo bricks while we ate Mom's cookies and played a wicked version of cutthroat Uno. Mom beat us all handily, and Jake whistled at her merciless tactics.

Matt headed home, and my parents helped Heather and Greg herd their kids to the car. Jake and I worked side by side in the kitchen, loading the dishes into the dishwasher.

"I got tasked to go to Sun Storm," Jake said as I handed him a plate.

I looked at him with raised eyebrows. "You know I have no idea what that means, right?"

"It's a huge training exercise held every year at Nellis." Jake arranged a dish in the rack and reached for a stack of dirty glasses.

"Nellis is the base in Vegas?" I asked.

"Yeah," he said. He glanced at me sideways. "It's for three weeks."

"Seriously?" My shoulders slumped. I turned off the water and grabbed a towel.

Jake nodded.

"I'm finally done with all my reports, I get eight weeks off, and now you have to leave?" My voice didn't hide my disappointment. I turned my back to the sink and leaned against the counter.

"I'm sorry," Jake said. "I was hoping I wouldn't have to go."

"Any chance things will change?" I asked hopefully.

"There's always a chance. That's the one constant in the military . . . change," he said, and a corner of his mouth lifted in a sympathetic grin.

"It's okay," I said and touched his arm. "I know it's out of your control."

"It is." Jake dried his hands. "But, Paige, it's always going to be this way. As long as I'm in the military, there's a large part of my life I don't control. Are you okay with that?"

His question was loaded with many layers and assumptions. My mind froze as I sifted through the possibilities. "What are you saying?" I finally asked.

"This is my life right now." Jake's eyes pierced mine, the blue pulling me in like the warm afternoon sun. "You know how I feel. I want you in my life, but I won't lie and tell you that moving forward will be easy." I tilted my head, and he reached forward and trailed his fingers down my arm. We laced our fingers together, and Jake held on to my hands while he wrapped his arms around my back. "I wish you could come with me. Three weeks is way too long to be away from you."

We stood leaning in to each other until Dad entered the room and coughed loudly. Jake chuckled and released me, and we moved back to the sink to finish our task.

The last time I saw Jake before his training mission was at his father's. Lucy had kindly included me in an invitation for dinner. I brought a plate of Mom's cookies and a green salad. Lucy whipped up a yummy chicken alfredo with french bread.

Jake's absence would affect Lucy and his dad more than me. He and Lucy worked hard to keep Mr. Summers busy. Jake's dad had finally allowed them to sort through Patty's effects, and her half of the closet now sat empty. Jake's dad got up every morning and went about his day, but his heart still weighed heavily with grief.

Still, the evening was casual and light. After the dishes were cleared, Lucy pulled out some old photo albums and showed me a picture of Jake in his tap shoes. Mr. Summers listened to his kids share stories and didn't add much. But he did smile a lot, and it warmed my heart.

Jake needed to finish packing, so I didn't stay long. He walked me to my car, and I promised myself I wouldn't get emotional. It was three weeks. Mandy had lasted three months—and she and Brandon had been engaged at the time! I could last three weeks.

"When can I call you?" I asked.

"I don't know. Sometimes we fly all night, and we won't know our schedule until the day before. We usually only fly every other day because of crew rest requirements, but we're constantly on alert." Jake leaned against my car and wrapped his arms around me. "It's part of the drill to test our flexibility and ability to respond, so I can't say for sure. I promise to call whenever I can," he said.

I made a pouty face.

"Hey, the good thing is I get to stay at the Bellagio instead of on base," Jake said. "At least I'll get a nice room."

"I'll miss you," I said.

"I'll miss you too. And I'll miss doing this." Jake leaned forward and kissed me sweetly. "Don't forget," he said while he held me close, "I love you."

I laughed in a pathetic attempt to make myself feel better. "It's only three weeks. I won't forget."

Then the moment came. Jake's eyes met mine, and there was nothing else that mattered in the whole world besides telling him the words thundering through my heart.

"Jake . . . I love you too."

The most handsome smile spread across his lips before he pressed them again to mine.

He pulled away, and a serious expression spread through his features. "I might forget."

"What?" I asked, confused.

"What you just said." Jake's dimple appeared.

"I love you," I repeated with a smile.

"I'm glad," Jake said.

I tried to say, "Me too," but Jake kissed me again, and it was the kind of kiss that left no need for words.

On the last day of school, Mandy invited me to dinner with her and Brandon.

"He's perfected his grilling, and tonight is salmon. Come on," Mandy said. "It's better than going home and moping."

"I'm not moping," I said defensively from my desk. Mandy stood in the middle of my empty room, crossed her arms, and scoffed. "Okay, maybe I'm moping a bit," I said. "But it's only been three days. How am I going to survive three weeks?" My arms were folded on my desk, and I dropped my head on top of them.

"Didn't Jake tell you where he was staying?" Mandy asked.

I lifted my head only slightly from the table. "Yeah, the Bellagio. Why?"

Mandy shrugged and sauntered over to my desk. She picked up my apple-adorned calendar, a teacher gift from the previous year, and pointed to the following week. "Let's see, I think this week's schedule is completely blank." She slid her finger down the page. "And this week too." I lifted my head slowly the rest of the way until I sat upright once again. Mandy pinned me with her dark eyes. "School's out, Paige. I think you need a Vegas getaway."

"You want me to go to Vegas?" I asked, putting all of my uncertainty into the question, because somewhere inside a little ember lit at Mandy's suggestion.

"I'm sure there's space at the Bellagio," Mandy said with a wicked smile.

"I don't gamble, Mandy, and I'm not talking about casinos. Last time I tried to surprise a guy, it didn't work out too well," I reminded her.

"Gavin's an idiot," Mandy said, and I smiled in agreement. "I can tell things are different with Jake. You know they are."

"Yeah, but to fly out there . . . His schedule's really busy. I mean, I've only talked to him once in three days." The desire to go burned warmer. I needed the rational side of my mind to keep my fluttery heart in check. "He's working. I can't just show up."

"You said he gets every other day off." Mandy shrugged again. "It was just a thought."

I'd read *The Adventures of Tom Sawyer*, and I knew how reverse psychology worked. I moaned and said, "If I say I'll come to dinner, will you change the topic?"

Mandy pasted on her best smile. "Do you want to bring a dessert?"

"Sure." I would pick up ice cream on the way.

I should have realized Brandon would side with his wife. As a team they were relentless. Seventy-two hours later, I boarded my flight for Vegas.

CHAPTER 27
I Gambled

I HADN'T BEEN TO VEGAS since I was thirteen and one of my friends had invited me to join her on a family trip. The highlight of that visit was our day spent at Circus Circus playing carnival games and watching the trapeze artists flip through the air. I had never had an interest in gambling. The odds always outweighed the reward, at least in monetary terms. I hoped my gamble for this trip would prove profitable.

When the taxi driver pulled under the expansive portico of the Bellagio, I exited with wide eyes. I'd expected to be wowed, but I'd had no idea the hotel housed an entire city. Shops with everything from food and books to clothing and gadgets lined the hallways. There were multiple pools, indoor mini-golf, spas, and of course the shows and slots.

I thought surprising Jake would be easy, but of course it wasn't. The woman at the front desk rebuffed my request and wouldn't provide his room number. When I explained my spontaneous trip and desire to surprise him, she gave me a false smile and offered to leave a message for him, but she still refused to share his information. I understood the whole privacy thing, but I wanted to surprise him, not leave a lame message. I began to doubt I would be able to locate him in the massive hotel.

The trek to my room included multiple long hallways, an elevator ride to the seventeenth floor, and lots of stops along the way to make sure I continued in the right direction.

The room housed all the features of a regular hotel: a king-sized bed, desk, mini-fridge, and bathroom, plus an amazing view. The decor mixed muted grays with dark blue and cream accents.

I unpacked and continued my exploration of the hotel while I decided how best to find Jake. I considered staking out the entrance but quickly realized there were too many doors for me to monitor. I could enlist Lucy as an accomplice to covertly get his room number, but I hadn't told her I was coming and felt it would now make for an awkward conversation. By the time darkness fell, I'd resigned myself to a solitary dinner. The pasta tasted great, but my initial high had deflated.

It had taken Mandy and Brandon a lot of persuading to convince me to come. I knew Jake was different from Gavin. When Jake said he loved me, I didn't doubt, and I reciprocated wholly. Gavin's pronouncement of love seemed sincere, but looking back, I'd been hungry for affirmation of his feelings. I'd pushed him too hard, which didn't excuse his cheating, but it had made my approach to things with Jake very different. I knew I loved Jake long before he'd professed to love me, but my contentment and peace with our relationship had allowed me to be patient. When Jake had finally revealed his heart, it had been without duress. It was simple, pure, and true, and that made his love different from anything I had ever been blessed with before.

Vegas signified the first solitary vacation I'd taken. Mandy and I had road-tripped, and my family always headed somewhere for summer break or a long holiday, but this bold move left me entirely alone. I didn't want to disappoint Mandy, so I only texted her the basics: amazing hotel, yummy dinner, no sign of Jake. I didn't receive a reply before dozing off for the night with my curtain open, watching the airplanes circle the Las Vegas skyline and wondering if Jake was looking at the same bright lights.

The sun brought renewed determination. I met with the concierge and easily made a list of all the attractions I did *not* want to see. Then I bought a map and plotted all of the nearby sights I did want to see. I feared if I wandered too far from the hotel, I would never find Jake.

I planned to explore two nearby hotels, but after navigating Caesars Palace for nearly four hours, I was beat. I headed back to the Bellagio, determined to enjoy one of the many hot tubs.

I entered the large main doors and decided to try again to persuade the front desk to give me some information. A man helped me this time, and after explaining my plight, I offered my best look of desperation. "Is there any information you can give me?"

"We can't give out our guests' reservation information," the man said. "But . . ." He quickly scanned to see if his coworkers were paying attention. He leaned slightly forward and said, "I can tell you that about thirty minutes ago a large group of military personnel was dropped off by a shuttle from the base."

I sighed. "He's probably crashed in his room watching hockey."

"Hockey?" The employee repeated. "One of them did ask where he could watch the hockey playoffs. I recommended our on-site sports bar." The man quickly grabbed a map and, with his pen, pointed to the location of the restaurant.

I glanced at the man's name tag. "Thank you, Patrick," I said. "You've been very helpful."

I oriented myself on the map and arrived at the sports bar a few minutes later, smoothing my clothes as I searched for Jake. I'd brought a special outfit for when I found him, but I didn't want to miss him because of a change of clothes, so my current attire would have to suffice. It totally made sense that Jake would be in the sports bar. He'd told me all about the playoffs, and my quickened heartbeat told me I'd finally found him.

After a quick scan I didn't notice anyone in military uniform. I bit my lip and wandered farther inside. There was no sign of Jake, but I would not be deterred. I circled the entire restaurant three times. Nothing. Disappointment shot through me, and I returned to my room.

I never made it to the hot tub. Instead I berated myself and my stupid logic that coming here would somehow be a good idea. I didn't gamble, I hated the smell of cigarette smoke, and now I'd wasted a good amount of money on a snazzy hotel room that I could sit in and feel lonely. My eyes moistened, but I refused to cry. Instead I sprawled across the giant bed and took a nap.

I woke groggily as the orange sun kissed the western horizon. My stomach rumbled. I grabbed the room-service menu, and while I flipped through it, gawking at the prices, I turned on the television. I mindlessly scrolled through channels with one hand while I read the description of a fifty-dollar meal, and my stomach grumbled again.

My thumb repetitively pressed the up arrow, and suddenly a channel caught my attention. I looked up to see two announcers comparing the pros and cons of the hockey teams skating on the ice behind them. One announcer wrapped up his assessment of the team with the happy words that the game would be starting in fifteen minutes.

I jumped off the bed and tossed the room-service menu onto the desk. Of course Jake wasn't at the sports bar earlier. The game hadn't been on. Somehow that important bit of information had completely eluded me.

Ignoring my rumbling stomach, I sorted through my suitcase and pulled out the outfit I had brought for this moment. The print on the sundress was bold, bright florals, and I'd bought a cute short-sleeved red cardigan to wear with it. I applied a fresh coat of makeup and swiped lip gloss across my smiling lips.

After a final check in the full-length mirror, I grabbed my phone off the bed and saw a missed call from Jake. He hadn't left a message, but the butterflies inside my belly fluttered around happily. He'd taken time to call me before heading down to watch the game. The timing of his call seemed to be a confirmation that he would be there, and I couldn't wait.

I stopped around the corner from the restaurant and took a deep breath. Jake would be surprised. I pictured the moment he saw me, his eyes widening with happy amusement, his mouth lifting in his adorable dimpled grin.

With determination I stepped through the fluorescent archway. It took a moment for my eyes to adjust to the dim light inside, but when I saw a group of about fifteen people staring up at the game projected on the flat-screen, I knew where to go.

I smiled at a couple sitting at a table and almost winked at the bartender. My uncontrollable glee only increased as I neared. Then I saw Jake.

A smile touched my lips as I watched him laugh. I'd told Mandy the truth; I was okay when Jake was away, but life felt so much more complete when I could reach out and touch him.

I'd pictured my interaction with Jake but hadn't considered an audience of his coworkers. The anticipation built like a whirlpool inside me. The feeling was intoxicating, but I also wanted it to be sucked away. A tiny niggling of uncertainty slowed my progression.

Jake wore his signature jeans with a collared shirt and Vans. His back was to me as he watched the game, and when I was three feet away, my feet froze. "Jake," I said far too softly for him to hear. I took a breath and tried again louder. "Jake."

He didn't turn around, but the dark-haired female who stood on his left side did. She eyed me up and down, and I unconsciously shifted my weight and offered a small smile.

She tilted her head toward Jake and laid a hand on his arm as she said something to him. Jake turned his head and gave her a look of confusion. Her eyes flicked toward me, and Jake finally turned all the way around.

My smile grew wide. "Hi," I said, lifting my right hand in a wave.

Jake squinted as if he were looking directly at the sun, and he shook his head in disbelief. "Paige?" He looked at the female standing next to him and then back at me. "What are you doing here?" he asked.

I opened my mouth, ready to shout some grand declaration. I'd thought through several scenarios in my head, and in every one, Jake's mouth had turned up into a happy smile. But looking at me now, Jake didn't smile. He didn't move. He stood there looking like someone had struck him over the head with a frying pan.

I took a shaky breath. "I . . . I wanted to surprise you," I said. Amid Jake's hesitation, it was the grandest declaration I could utter. My arms lifted from my side, then fell flatly back down.

The hockey game must not have been very interesting, because at that point Jake's entire group turned to watch the entertainment my appearance provided. Jake's usual decisiveness was vacant, and when he looked again at the woman standing next to him, it almost appeared like he was asking her opinion. No words were exchanged, but the beautiful brunette gave him a pointed look of displeasure.

Jake opened his mouth, looked around again, then stepped toward me before finally speaking again. "When did you get here?" He put his hand on my upper arm and turned me away from his gawking companions.

"Yesterday," I said softly. "You said you wished I could come . . ." I reached over to touch him but stopped as the whirlpool inside began sucking away my courage.

"When I said that, I didn't think you'd actually come," Jake said.

My courage completely fled, and I folded my arms across my chest to cover the emptiness I felt inside. "You said you had some downtime. I figured we could sightsee or something."

He glanced behind us, and I followed his gaze. Everyone had turned back to the game—except the woman. Her hot glare burned like a branding iron. I pressed my eyes closed and focused on the waves of conversation floating across the tables. If in the blackness I could pick out the happy words of another patron or sort through the noise to hear the words of the song playing in the background, then I wouldn't focus on the irritation in Jake's eyes or the frustration in his voice.

He touched me again. I flinched, and my eyes flew open.

His eyes grew more distant. They retreated somewhere inside him, and he no longer looked at me like a man in love. "Paige, this is a work trip. It's not a vacation," he said.

I couldn't help it; I outright laughed, and something inside me snapped. "Then, I'll let you get back to work. I can see you're really busy defending freedom, watching hockey, and flirting with your coworkers." I fisted my fingers at my side.

Jake started to protest. "Paige, I—"

"Jake?" The brunette walked up beside him. She stood so close her shoulder touched Jake's arm. Apparently sending killer looks didn't suffice. She wanted to personally stick the dagger into my heart. "Everything okay?" she asked with feigned innocence.

The muscle in Jake's jaw tightened, but he didn't speak; I did.

"Hi, I'm Paige." I extended my hand.

The woman looked at my hand like it was a dead fish, but then she gripped it firmly. "Callie," she said.

"Everything's fine," I said. "I guess I misunderstood something Jake told me a few weeks ago." Callie looked at him with a question in her eyes, but I was not about to stop to let him answer. "You guys enjoy the game. And Jake"—I looked at him, and my heart began a free fall—"it was good seeing you. I'm sorry the feeling wasn't mutual."

It took every ounce of strength I had to turn and walk away. But I did it, proud my voice didn't break. The same was not true for my heart.

CHAPTER 28
I Hid

FORTUNATELY, FLYING OUT OF LAS Vegas on a Tuesday evening was a rarity, and the airline willingly changed my flight without charging me any additional fees. I had to take a loss for the hotel room, but after Jake's rejection, I saw no reason to stay. I wanted to go home, climb into bed, and hide away from the world.

When I'd fled the sports bar, I'd thought I heard Jake call my name. He may have even followed, but I'd learned my lesson. Never try to surprise a boyfriend. Ever. I'd melted into the crowd exiting one of the shows and taken a very long detour. The moment I slipped through the door to my room, Jake had started blowing up my phone. He tried to call half a dozen times, then switched to texts.

Where are you?

Can we PLEASE talk?

Let me explain.

Paige, please tell me your room number. The front desk won't give it to me.

I laughed at the irony, then responded. *I know. It took me two days to find you. I'm going home.*

One more text arrived before I powered down my phone. *Please don't leave.*

His words tugged at my heart, but my bruises burned too fresh. I shut off my phone and unplugged the hotel phone from the wall for good measure. Then I packed my suitcase and weaved through the smoky casino exit to hail a cab.

Once I landed back in California, I ignored all the texts and phone messages screaming at me to be read and heard and called Matt to come pick me up. I figured my brother would ask the least amount of questions.

I figured right. After explaining why I came back early, Matt only said, "Too bad, sis. I liked Jake."

"Me too," I said, and then I stared out the window until we pulled into my driveway.

The next morning at ten a.m. sharp, my doorbell rang. I looked through the peephole to see an armful of stargazer lilies. The sight made me freeze until the doorbell sounded again, and I opened the door to sign for the delivery. The kid insisted he wasn't allowed to accept a tip and quickly retreated to his car.

I set the lilies down and stared at the card for a long time, debating whether or not I should read it. Jake was fighting, and it made moping extremely difficult. My emotions were like a switch, flipping back and forth between anger and tendresse. The scales weren't balanced at all, and the continuous jostle made me light-headed.

I'd seen Jake with Callie. I'd seen the way she touched him and watched him and claimed him as hers. Yet, for as many times as I'd replayed the scene in my head, I knew Jake didn't reciprocate her affection. I'd seen his eyes light and his grin turn upward for me for weeks. None of that had happened with Callie. He didn't touch her back or acknowledge her as more than a colleague. I couldn't take offense there. My problem stemmed from his cold reception. He may not have shown any sort of affection for Callie, but he also hadn't shown any for me.

I needed time to sort out my feelings, to decide what I wanted. My heart urged me to open the card, hoping the sentimental flowers were an apology. But I didn't want Jake to apologize for something he wasn't sorry for. I didn't want to force him to feel something he didn't. His profession of love had come wholly from him, and I'd considered it a treasure, a reward for my patience, a sign from above that Jake was the right path. But maybe I'd been mistaken. Maybe I had pressured him in some way. The one thing I couldn't get out of my head was the dismayed look on Jake's face when he'd seen me standing in the restaurant. If he truly loved me, why hadn't he been happy to see me?

I left the card attached to the bouquet and went for a run. Every time my thoughts turned to Jake, I sprinted until my lungs cried for a break. My lungs hurt a lot over the next hour.

After a long warm shower and a bowl of oatmeal, I decided to read the card. Jake hadn't texted anymore. I assumed whatever he wanted to say was scrawled across the tiny card, although Lucy would have transcribed his message. I realized I was being theatrical, but I couldn't help it. My heart skittered all over the place, ducking in the shadow of doubt, bumping around in a search for courage, speeding and slowing as I couldn't determine what I hoped to find within the small cream-colored envelope.

I slowly plucked the card free and walked away from the alluring scent of the lilies. Sitting down at my kitchen table, I read:

You promised honesty, and so did I. Here goes . . .

My heartbeat quickened with fear, but I returned my eyes to the card.

There are some changes coming in my life, and we need to talk. Please call me. Jake

Such simple words, yet they were loaded. The weight of the unknown squeezed my heart. The contradiction between what I wanted and what had happened in Vegas lay on the forefront of my mind. *Changes*—the vagueness of the word, the infinite possibilities, spread like a plaque because my glass was no longer half-full. It was empty.

I reached for my phone. I needed clarification. I desperately wanted to hear Jake's voice, his confidence flowing through his words to convince me of their truthfulness. Maybe it would be better to speak over the phone. Looking in his eyes, I would be unable to concentrate on the words coming out of his mouth. And being hundreds of miles apart, he couldn't persuade me with a kiss or a quirk of his lips. He would have to use words and logic and common sense. I needed common sense. Emotions were too messy, and mine were jaded by all things Jake.

My finger hovered over the call button until I finally pressed it. One ring. Two. The silence in the house begged to be broken. Three. Four. Then . . . voicemail.

I listened to Jake's easy voice ask me to leave a message, and then I ended the call.

Before I could think about my reaction, I called Heather and asked if I could watch her kids for the night. After an explanation of why I was back in California, she sounded like she wanted to ask more questions, but instead she accepted my offer.

I scrubbed my house from top to bottom, ate three bowls of cereal around four, then left for Heather's. Her house smelled amazing, and she told me she made cheesy pasta and breadsticks for the kids and me. Her homemade mac and cheese topped my list of favorites.

I gave her a tight squeeze. "You're the best sister ever," I said.

"I'm your only sister," she teased. "Just take care of my kids, okay? Bedtime is seven thirty, but Max has been pushing it, and Amelia thinks if she cries, she can stay up too. Nathaniel always goes down like a champ." I followed Heather through the house as she pointed out all the necessities. "Diapers, wipes, bottle, pacifier."

"I have done this a time or two," I said.

Greg walked into the living room. "Come on, Heather. The kids are going to have a great time with their aunt, and I'm sure she'll follow your schedule with precision." He winked at me.

She swatted his arm. "Paige knows I trust her. I just want to cover all the basics. You know how Amelia likes to test limits lately. Max too."

"We'll be fine. Go have fun." I picked Nathaniel up from his blanket on the floor and followed Greg and Heather to the door. "Don't hurry home. You have a cell phone, and I promise to call if I need anything."

Amelia ran up beside me, and we watched them pull away. "Let's play!" she said.

We played house, ate Heather's yummy food, and the kids all went to sleep with only minimal protests from Amelia. I texted a picture of three sleeping kids to Heather, bragging that it was only seven thirty-six.

Greg convinced Heather to make the most of their kid-free night, and after dinner they headed to see a new action movie. I scoured Heather's cabinets until I discovered her chocolate stash, and then I stretched out on the couch and searched for something to watch on TV.

About halfway through a reality show about flipping houses, my phone chimed with a text. *I'm sorry I missed your call. Just finished work. Are you still up?*

My stomach flipped, and the couch suddenly didn't feel very cozy. Was I ready to talk to Jake? I lowered my feet to the floor and responded vaguely. *I'm babysitting.*

Jake: *Can I call you?*

Another text chimed before I could reply. *Please?*

It seemed pointless to text my reply. I scrolled to Jake's name and dialed.

He picked up immediately. "Paige," he said. I heard him take a breath, but he only said, "Hi."

Any courage I might've had fled, and instead of talking about anything of consequence, I asked about work. Jake patiently replied, and then I could sense the hesitancy in his voice.

"Sounds like you made it home okay," he said.

"Yeah."

"I . . . I wish you wouldn't have left," Jake said. His voice grew softer. "I tried to find you."

I stood and walked to the back sliding door. The blackness staring back swallowed my confidence. "I had to leave," I said.

"Why?" he asked.

"Why?" I repeated with a short laugh. "Because my surprise didn't go quite like I had planned. Your reaction confirmed it was a bad idea. Did you really think I would stay?"

"I wanted you to stay," Jake said, his voice practically a whisper.

"That's not how it looked from my perspective." I pressed my eyes closed.

I heard Jake offer a heavy sigh on his end of the line, but he didn't say anything.

"Callie definitely didn't want me to stay," I said. The words were hard to say aloud, but we could only avoid it for so long. I felt as though a drop of acid were searing my heart, and I placed my free hand over my chest in a vain effort to control the pain.

"Paige." When Jake said my name, the sound was a combination of pleading and remorse. "I am so sorry for what happened. I wish I would have known you were coming, but not for the reasons you think. Some things happened the other day, and when you walked in, everything collapsed at once."

A flare of anger shot through me. "I don't want to hear this, Jake. Yes, I want honesty, but not like this. I don't need to hear about your change of feelings or some sudden realization that you don't care for me. If you want things to be over, say the word. Break my heart all at once, because this chipping away bits and pieces is much more excruciating." My chest heaved beneath my hand. My voice rose. "Man up. Tell me it's over, and then Callie can have you."

"This has nothing to do with Callie!" Jake said sharply. "She's a flirt who happens to be the mission commander of this trip. What happened to trust, Paige?"

"It kind of flew out the window the moment I walked into the sports bar. You stood there while she pawed all over you," I said.

"So you left because of Callie?" Jake groaned. "I didn't ask her to get involved. I didn't invite her advances. I thought you knew me better than that. I thought you trusted me."

"I did trust you, Jake. I flew all the way to Vegas because I trusted that when you said you wanted me to be there, you meant it. But you didn't," I said, and a tear slid down my cheek. "You made that abundantly clear."

"I wish I could see you. I wish I could take you in my arms and hold you and convince you how much I"—Jake's voice hitched—"I love you. I want to be with you and only you, Paige."

"Then, it's good you're not here," I said, although it was a complete lie. I wanted nothing more than to feel Jake's warm arms wrapped around me. He knew my weakness. He knew I couldn't resist him if he were standing before me. I wiped the moisture from my face and sniffed.

"Can I at least try to explain what happened that day?" Jake asked.

"Will it matter?" I asked. "Will it change anything?"

Jake groaned into the phone. "Nothing has changed. I love you."

Thundering silence dominated the phone line.

"I'm more certain of that than ever, Paige. My feelings haven't changed," he repeated. "Please tell me yours haven't either." A thread of unease paralleled his plea.

Oh, how I wanted to believe his words. I loved him too. I couldn't deny it. I wanted to echo the endearment back, but the scars on my heart kept my voice frozen.

"Don't give up on me, Paige. I'll be home in seven days," Jake said. "We'll talk then."

"Okay," I whispered.

"Seven days," Jake said again.

"Goodbye, Jake," I said in reply, and after I hung up, I wondered which of our final words would come true.

CHAPTER 29
I Understood

A NEW BOUQUET OF LILIES arrived every day after our phone call. Each arrangement included a note with a reference to a memory Jake and I had made together. My entire house smelled like a fragrant spring garden. The scent permeated the air, and I grew accustomed to the sweetness. Every time I returned home, the mellifluous scent reminded me of Jake's persistence and acted as a temporary splint on my heart.

Jake didn't text or call again. The days passed slowly, and I kept myself occupied by helping Mom complete her picture-scanning project. She provided me with lots of warm comfort food and offered to let me stay the night. I agreed but left early to make sure I arrived home in time to receive my delivery of lilies.

Wednesday afternoon I'd just returned home from a run when the doorbell rang. When I looked through the peephole, I saw more lilies held by a handsome delivery man with bright, hopeful blue eyes.

I hadn't known how I would react to seeing Jake, and in truth, I had tried to not give it much thought so I wouldn't be disappointed. But in the moment, my heart fluttered like crazy, and it scared me.

Despite my workout clothes and my sweaty hair, I opened the door.

Jake's lips tilted in a hopeful grin. "Hi, Paige." He shifted his weight to the right as he extended the flowers toward me. "These are for you."

I accepted the flowers and fingered the soft petals. A myriad of thoughts cycled through my mind. Should I let Jake through the door? Should I demand an explanation or ignore the oddness between us? Should I wait and say nothing at all? Or should I step forward and kiss him? I desperately wanted to.

In the end, Jake spoke first. "I guess I should have called. I just . . . I didn't want to wait. Is now a good time?"

My first reaction was to point out the danger of surprising someone, to remind him that surprises and I don't mix. But when I glanced down at my running capris and sweat-soaked workout tank, my sarcastic thoughts faded. I knew Jake and I needed to have this conversation, and I also knew I needed to shower to clear my head before I jumped into it.

"Can you give me thirty minutes?" I asked.

"Sure." Jake stuck his hands into his jean pockets. "Are you hungry? I could go grab some sandwiches from Millie's."

"Okay," I said.

"Okay," Jake repeated. Then he looked at his watch. "Take your time. I'll come back at ten forty-five."

I nodded my head in acknowledgment and slowly backed into the house and closed the door. I filled a vase for the new flowers and carried them with me to the bathroom. Multiple surfaces throughout the house were now covered with lilies, and the bathroom counter offered open space.

I showered, and as I stood in front of my closet debating my outfit choices, my thoughts sidetracked. Why did I want to look good for Jake? Was it because I wanted him to notice me? Did I want to make him jealous? Or maybe I wanted him to realize I was his perfect match, the one who would balance the scales and make life peaceful and stable.

I selected a flirty black skirt and a white lacy top layered over a hot-pink fitted tee. I pulled on my silver sandals and moved back to the bathroom to dry my hair. Anticipation roiled in my stomach, and I tried to concentrate on completing my daily routine. I spritzed my hair with spray gel and fingered through the loose waves while I blew it dry. My cheeks were red from the heat in my bathroom, so I only applied a light layer of eye shadow and mascara. Then I looked again at the lilies.

The scent of the hair products settled, and I inhaled the fragrant sweetness of the flowers. They were peaceful and perfect, exactly how life with Jake had been only weeks ago. But looking at the flowers, they didn't mock me. Instead they invited me to return to a place of comfort and simplicity. My breathing slowed as I remembered the starlit night at the lake. That moment had held an eternity for Jake and me. Our relationship felt invincible and sure. How had the feeling spiraled away so quickly?

I heard a knock and said a quick prayer for guidance. Then I moved to the front door and let Jake in. We offered each other a scant greeting, and Jake carried the bag of food to the table.

"Do you want to talk first or eat?" Jake asked.

I opted to eat. Avoidance was a technique I excelled at. But the anticipation of our impending conversation hung in the air like buzzing static. There was no reason to delay. Neither of us enjoyed our meal anyway, although Jake had remembered chicken salad was my favorite.

After we both picked at our food, I gave Jake a weak smile and conceded. "I guess we should talk."

He pushed his plate to the side and ran his hand over his short hair. He blew out a breath and said, "I hope you'll hear me out."

I nodded, folded my arms on the table, and vowed to keep eye contact with Jake. Whatever he said, I would know the truth of it if I could see his eyes.

"When my mom died, I knew things would change," Jake began, and I startled at his comment. Whatever I'd expected him to say, it was not related to his mother. "She was . . . so good." Jake's voice caught. "You saw firsthand how hard that was for me. I wallowed in my grief, questioned God, and pushed away all the wonderful and good things in my life, including you." His eyes brightened, and he stared at me in earnest sincerity. "When I realized I might lose you, something inside of me snapped. I knew I had to let go of my self-pity. If losing my mom hurt, losing you would be a thousand times worse."

"Jake," I cut in, but he didn't stop.

"I'm telling the truth, Paige." Jake reached across the table and put his warm hand over mine. "What happened to my mom was out of my control. I had to let her go. There was nothing I could do, and there's no way she would want me to remember her with sorrow. She was too happy a person for that." He tightened his hold on my hand. "But if I lost you, it would have been entirely my fault. I needed to stop focusing on my loss and focus on my joy. That's you, Paige—your smile, your kind heart, your patience—and I know I've tested every one of those great qualities. But you bring me so much happiness."

I had to look away then. Everything Jake said sounded too ideal, too perfect, and as expected, I could see the truth in his eyes. The adage Mom often repeated, that if something seemed too good to be true it probably was, rattled through me like a small tremor.

"You weren't happy in Vegas," I said while I stared at the smooth grain of the table.

"That day was really rough for me," Jake said.

"Me too," I added quickly and looked back at him, hoping he could read the pain in my eyes.

"I know. I'm sorry, Paige. In the cockpit I can react to threats or emergencies with calm precision. Obviously it's a skill I haven't developed in life." Jake moved his hand from mine, and I immediately wanted it back. "Like I said, I knew after Mom died things would change."

"Why are you changing the subject again?" I asked with desperation. "I'm sorry about your mom, Jake. You know I am. But we need to talk about us. We need to talk about what happened in Vegas, and if you don't want to discuss that, then we have nothing to say to each other."

He rested his elbows on the table and put his head in his hands. "I've been stationed at Travis for six years," he said, and then he raised his face to look at me again. "My commanders were sensitive to the fact that my mom was sick and helped me work the system to my advantage so I could remain stationed here. Now that Mom's passed, they no longer need to make an exception."

I narrowed my eyes and studied Jake's expression. It was the first time I had noticed the weariness in his gaze. The blue in his eyes was no longer an oasis but a sad rainstorm.

"I'm getting transferred, Paige."

I said nothing. In truth, I couldn't have spoken if I wanted to. My world felt off-kilter, and I feared if I spoke, the air from my breath would be enough to send it tumbling.

"I don't know exactly when it will happen, but I assume my new assignment will arrive in about a month and I'll be gone in less than six." Jake's eyes turned a shade darker. "I found out the day you surprised me in Vegas. When I arrived in the morning for my flight, I had an email from my commander. My dream sheet had to be completed by close of business, and I'd sent it in right before I went to the restaurant and saw you.

"Callie flew with me that day, and somehow she knew too. She's the director of operations, and she can have a lot of sway in determining new assignments. She uses her position to her advantage, and truthfully, her behavior borders on sexual harassment, but I swear I've never encouraged her. In fact, after you left the restaurant and I couldn't find you, I went straight to my room and called the schedulers. I persuaded them to stick me on the opposite shift from Callie for the rest of the exercise."

I looked down and saw my hands shaking. Jake followed my gaze and moved his arm as if to reach for me, but then he pulled back and took a deep breath. "Paige, when I saw you standing there, you were a ray of sunshine. I know it sounds cheesy, but it's true. I wanted so badly to pull you into my arms, but in the same instant I remembered I would also have to tell you I was leaving . . . and it felt like my heart had been trampled."

I'd been still for so long that something inside me snapped. The helplessness in Jake's eyes pricked my heart. I stood and stared at him. The connection between us was strong and real—more real than anything I had felt before—and I wondered how I could ever have doubted him. Guilt washed through me, and I turned away and walked to the living room window.

Jake followed, and as he stood beside me, I only wanted him to make good on his word to hold me in his arms.

He spoke softly. "I was a mess, and I know there's no excusing my behavior, but I want you to know why."

My mind teetered between compassion and fear. I finally understood. My anger at Jake had been misguided, and I realized I'd wasted time. Precious, limited time.

"I'm sorry," I cried out and turned to face him. "I promised you honesty, and when the time came that you needed my trust, I failed you. You were hurting that day, and instead of bringing you comfort, I brought you more pain." My eyes filled with tears.

"Oh, Paige," Jake said.

And then my wish came true. His arms wrapped around me, and he pulled me to him. I leaned in to his warm, solid chest, clutching my hands around his waist and wishing I could freeze the moment. We stood close, breathing in one another, and the world began to roll back into balance—until I remembered Jake was leaving.

I tilted my head to look at him. "What did you put on your wish list?" I whispered.

He looked down at me and raised one hand to the side of my face. "My first choice is to stay here," he said.

My heart instantly lifted. "Is that possible?"

"It's not impossible." He shrugged.

"Where else could you go?" I asked.

"Washington is my second choice, then New Jersey." Jake's thumb brushed my cheek.

"I don't want you to go," I said, and the wounds on my heart burned fresh.

"I know." Jake tightened his hold on me again and buried his nose in my hair. "I know."

Then he began to chuckle. I lifted my chin to make eye contact again. "What?"

"Does this mean I'm forgiven?" Jake asked.

I untangled my hands from his waist and repositioned them behind his neck. He must have read the mischievous look in my eye because his mouth split into a grin right before I pulled him to me and pressed my lips to his.

He reacted immediately, kissing me back. His fingers threaded through my hair, and his lips caressed mine, firm and tender. After a lingering moment, we pulled apart. "Does that answer your question?" I asked.

Jake feigned innocence. His lips pulled to one side, and he gave me a dubious look. "Nope," he said. "You'd better tell me again."

So I did.

CHAPTER 30
I Hoped

THE MONTH OF JULY PASSED in a blur. Jake and I knew his assignment would arrive any day, but neither of us talked about it. We weren't naive enough to think it wouldn't happen; we knew it would, but it was easier to push the truth aside than to deal with it. Jake's plane was stationed at various bases around the world. I hoped he would be assigned to stay in the United States and hoped even more that he would remain at Travis Air Force Base.

Summer break meant my days were wide open, and whenever Jake wasn't working, we were together. I wondered if we both secretly wanted to store away as many memories as possible because deep down we knew those memories would be limited.

Sometimes Jake planned something extravagant, but most of the time our outings were simple. We ate lots of dinners with his dad and took a day trip to the beach and another to San Francisco. Jake asked me to help paint his condo near the base, and although neither of us said it, I knew it was so it would be ready to rent out if he moved.

We watched fireworks over the lake while waving sparklers in the air, went on a double date with Mandy and Brandon, and played cards with my parents, and one Saturday morning we manned Lucy's booth at the farmer's market because she was shorthanded. Jake plucked a stargazer lily from the bucket, broke off the stem, and stuck it into my hair. The message of peace he associated with the flower practically floated into my head. After all the turbulence, life with Jake was peaceful. We ignored the gathering clouds, the lightning and thunder, and the impending storm brewing on the horizon.

The moments compounded quickly; the memories built easily, one upon another.

My mom warned me I was falling too hard, too deep. I knew she was right, but I ignored her. I was too happy to believe it could all end. I harbored hope that Jake wouldn't get transferred at all, that somehow those in charge would realize Jake's mission was best fulfilled in sunny California. I prayed for God to intervene, to allow the blessing of Jake to continue in my life. The hardest part of those prayers was asking God to help me accept whatever He had planned.

Jake had made a habit of calling me the moment he walked out the door of his office. We'd talk about his day and then make plans to see each other. Then came the afternoon when four thirty passed, then five, and five thirty, and Jake still hadn't called.

Of course, I had quickly learned that missions, schedules, and routines in the military changed without notice. I worried about him flying when we'd been out late, and some of the stories he'd shared made me realize how dangerous his job really was. But somehow, that day, there was no doubt in my mind; I knew his delay in calling me was not related to an aircraft problem or a sudden mission assignment. I knew he had received his new orders. The problem with this sure knowledge was it also meant those orders were not for Travis Air Force Base, California. If they were, Jake would have called.

I had fallen into the pattern of pushing away the inevitable, and while I trusted Jake, I couldn't completely forget his propensity to close up. He'd turned to me during the rough times, and we'd worked through roadblocks together, but I worried that the longer he kept to himself, the higher the wall around his emotions would grow. I needed to find him.

I called Lucy, then Mr. Summers, casually asking if they'd heard from Jake. Since I'd constantly been at his side, I'm sure they figured out my true purpose. My efforts were fruitless. After calling Jake twice and not receiving a reply, I texted. *Hey, handsome—where are you?*

Jake didn't reply for about fifteen minutes, during which time I paced my living room floor and then attempted to watch TV but instead busted my remote when I threw it down on the coffee table in frustration. So I paced again. Finally, my phone chimed.

Jake: *Can I pick you up in one hour?*

Me: *Um . . . sure.*

Jake: *Dress for outdoors—Love you.*

Jake told me he loved me often enough that I didn't wonder whether it was true. Never had he put it in a text, and my mind automatically scrolled through possible explanations of why he did now. The only reason I could come up with was that he did get his orders, he would be moving away soon, and he wanted to fit in as many reminders of his feelings as he could.

In my heart, I knew something had happened, but I tried not to linger on those emotions. Instead I focused on the joy I felt to realize Jake was not erecting his walls. It may have taken a little prodding—two phone calls and a text, to be exact—but he'd responded, so I counted it a success.

I grabbed a gray long-sleeved scoop-neck tee that would easily slip over my tank top, then left my green fleece pullover on the arm of the couch to wait. It was overkill for a summer night in California, but I figured I would cover all the bases.

Then I paced some more.

Eating would have been a good idea. My stomach nagged at me to fill it, but then it churned when I wondered what news Jake was going to share. I settled the tug-of-war by shoving a handful of crackers into my mouth.

Finally, the doorbell rang. I took a deep breath before answering. Jake wore jeans, a button-down shirt, and a pair of black Vans. His lips twitched, but his stance was solid. My pacing had been anything but solid.

"Hi," I said.

"Hi," Jake echoed.

"Everything okay?"

"Yeah." Jake nodded. "You ready?"

I cocked my head and studied Jake. His face appeared relaxed, peaceful. The calm in his eyes calmed my nerves. I took another breath, and my heart settled into a steady rhythm. "Yeah."

Jake eyed my armful of clothes. "It looks like you're a well-prepared Boy Scout," he said.

"Options are a good thing." I shrugged. Jake's playful mood amused me. I still felt confident that his new assignment had arrived, and I wondered if I'd gotten it wrong. Maybe he was staying in California. I let the hope percolate.

When we got to the car and Jake opened the door, the delicious smell of pizza hit me. I inhaled deeply, and Jake noticed. Laughing, he said, "I'll feed you soon. We're not going far. I promise."

It was almost eight o'clock, and the sun began to droop on the western horizon. Jake refused to tell me where he was taking me. He hummed along with the song on the radio, and every once in a while he would spit out some random fact. He was perfectly chill.

I, on the other hand, was an antsy mess. At home I'd been nervous; once Jake had arrived, I'd calmed down. Now, watching him casually spout facts about boy bands and weather cycles, my emotions couldn't keep up. I liked a mellow Jake, and I also liked his steadiness. But tonight he was unpredictable.

He wound through a neighborhood, and when the houses grew farther and farther apart, the land filled with vineyards. We turned down a gravel road, surrounded by rows of grapes sprawled out along parallel wire trellises. Jake slowed and then stopped altogether in the middle of a field.

I looked at him with raised brows.

He inhaled deeply, then reached over, squeezed my hand, and got out of the car.

His cryptic signs were killing me. He retrieved the pizza from the back seat, opened my door, and handed me the food. Then he grabbed another bag and a blanket and retook my free hand before leading me to a path of paver stones that wound through the vineyard.

I followed along, my stomach still pinging and buzzing. I was both curious and mystified, and the combination left me silent. There was too much static in my head for me to form words anyway.

Jake pulled me forward and then stepped to my side. The sky opened up, and I caught my breath. We stood in a large circular clearing. Leafy green vines surrounded every side, and there were no other obvious paths. In the center of the circle sat three small couches surrounding a deeply dug firepit. Behind one of the couches was a rectangular metal table with eight chairs, but it was currently arranged with place settings for two. Two plates, two fluted glasses, and two tall candlesticks sat on either side of the centerpiece—a bursting bouquet of stargazer lilies.

Words still would not transfer to my mouth.

Jake walked to the table, and I followed and set the pizza down. The sprawling vines blocked our vision of the lowering sun, but Jake looked up at the periwinkle sky. Then he looked back at me. His eyes danced in excitement.

"Should we eat?" he asked.

He began to rummage through the bag he'd brought until he fished out a lighter. Once both candles glowed, he clicked it off and set it aside.

"Jake, what are you up to? How did you . . . ? Where are we?" I began, but my questions were curtailed as Jake put a finger over my lips.

"Shhh," he whispered. "Let's eat, and I will reveal all my secrets in due time." He grinned at my perplexed look.

He held my chair and served my pizza with ridiculous flair. "My lady," he said and placed a slice of Hawaiian yumminess in front of me.

I smirked at his exaggerated chivalry and took a bite. The warm cheese was heavenly, and I stuffed my mouth so full I could only murmur my appreciation.

Jake kept my plate filled with pizza and my glass filled with sparkling cider. We smiled and ate, and words were a minimum. As the sky grew darker, Jake moved to the firepit, and after lighting the fire, he tossed log after log into the pit until he'd worked the flame to a roaring blaze.

"Are you sure you won't catch the vineyard on fire?" I asked and stood to move closer to the warmth of the flames.

"I've been assured that won't happen," he said.

He walked behind me and pulled my back to his chest. We stared at the burning wood, the comforting smell of the campfire floating around us as the stars began to peek out overhead.

"Come here," Jake said and led me to one of the couches. We sat down, and I rested my head on his shoulder. "We fly over this place all the time," he said. "The running joke is it's a crop circle left by the aliens. But I was always curious about this clearing, so I did a little research and got in contact with the owner about a year ago. He invited me to come check it out. It was pretty cool; his whole family showed up to meet me and thank me for my service. They said I was welcome back anytime, but this is the first time I've taken them up on the offer."

"I'm a lucky girl," I mused, acknowledging the truth of my words. I twisted my neck to look up at Jake.

He shifted his arm around my back and began to play with the ends of my hair. I turned my focus to the fire, but I felt him looking at me.

Finally, Jake spoke again. "My orders came today."

Peace slipped away, and nerves bounded through my belly. I leaned against his shoulder again. "I wondered . . . when you didn't call me."

His breath skimmed the top of my head, but he said nothing more.

The flame fluctuated between orange and red, dancing across the wood to the crackling rhythm. The heat fell over us like a warm blanket, and as content as I was to sit in Jake's arms, I needed to know.

"Well?" I asked.

After another breath Jake shifted until we faced one another. He took my hands in his. "Paige, they're sending me to New Jersey," he said calmly. Too calmly.

The ideal was for Jake to stay in California. Even a transfer to Washington seemed manageable, but New Jersey? The Atlantic Ocean was so far away. Despair filled my heart drip by drip as I tracked the miles in my mind.

"Paige?" Jake called my name, and I looked back into his eyes. They didn't mirror the gloom I felt. "You know I love you."

"Yes, but New Jersey? I don't know, Jake."

"Don't know if you want to stay together?" His eyes narrowed, and he watched me.

"Of course I do," I said, and his eyes brightened. "I'm just scared."

"Why?"

"Because I love you too, and I don't want to lose you." The fire now felt suffocating. I stood and walked back to the table.

Jake followed me, and when he reached the table, he pulled a single stargazer lily from the bunch. He walked close and handed it to me. "You won't lose me," he said.

I took the flower and twirled it in my fingers. "New Jersey's really far away, and we won't get to see each other very often." I inhaled a shaky breath. "How can you be sure?"

"Because I want you to come with me," Jake said.

The fuzzy smoke rising from the fire melted into the sky, and time shifted to slow motion.

My eyes rose to his. "What?"

Jake took my free hand in his. "You're right. New Jersey is too far away, and I don't want to be away from you. Ever." He dropped down on one knee, and the pinging in my heart turned to bursting fireworks. "Paige, I've felt this is right for a while now. No matter where my orders sent me, I knew I wanted you there too. You are my happiness. You are my peace. You are my forever. Will you marry me?"

My vocabulary vanished. I was in a state of joyful shock and couldn't manage even a one-word answer.

Jake's eyes turned from hopeful to uncertain. He began playing with my fingers. "I know I'm asking a lot," he said. "Your family's here. Your job is here. Your life is here."

"That's not true," I said, quickly finding my voice. "My life . . . my happiness is with you." Jake's face erupted into a dimpled smile. "Yes," I said and tugged on his hand until he stood up. "I love you, Jake Summers." I threw my arms around his neck. "And I want nothing more than to become your wife."

Jake kissed me then. It was a kiss filled with promise, passion, and a hope for eternity. It represented a complete balance of everything we felt for one another.

Jake pulled back with a contented sigh. "I love you," he whispered in my ear. "You know me well enough to know my weaknesses. You know how my career works. I can't promise stability, but I can promise to cherish you forever."

"I'll take it." I smiled up at him.

Then his eyes widened, and he released his hold on me. "I almost forgot." He reached into his pocket and pulled out a simple gold ring with a round-cut diamond. I beamed and raised my left hand. He slipped the ring over my finger and said, "If you want to choose your own ring, I'll take you shopping. But this one belonged to my mother, and I thought maybe—"

"It's beautiful," I said, staring at the diamond glistening against the dancing flame of the fire. My breath froze, and my heart filled with humility. "Are you sure, Jake?"

"I think somehow she knew you were perfect for me." He lifted my hand to his lips and kissed it.

"What did I do to deserve you?" I asked.

"You returned your shopping cart," Jake said as he pulled me into one of his warm, perfect hugs.

Best. Decision. Ever.

ABOUT THE AUTHOR

CHALON LINTON HAS BEEN A military spouse for twenty-plus years. Through eight deployments and multiple moves, she has met amazing people and established a network of forever friends around the world. She writes from a place of respect and awe, combining her love for romance with her appreciation for the patriots who sacrifice daily to defend freedom.

You can learn more about Chalon's books at chalonlinton.com.

Twitter: @LizzyLint26

Instagram: lintonloveslife

Facebook: Author Chalon Linton